JENNY
Beach Brides Series

by
Melissa McClone

Jenny (Beach Brides Series)
Copyright © 2017 Melissa McClone

Cover Design by Raine English
Elusive Dreams Designs
www.ElusiveDreamsDesigns.com

Content Editing by Mary-Theresa Hussy
Good Stories Well Told
www.goodstorieswelltold.com

Copyediting by Cynthia Shepp
Editing Services by Cynthia Shepp
www.cynthiashepp.com

Cardinal Press, LLC
First Digital Edition, June 2017
ISBN-13: 978-1-944777-01-2

DEDICATION

For my online besties Denise, Kimberly, and Tina who are in touch daily and keep me going!

And to my amazing virtual assistant Cindy Jackson who is only an email away when I need help!

INTRODUCTION

Grab your beach hat and a towel and prepare for a brand new series brought to you by twelve *New York Times* and *USA Today* bestselling authors...

Beach Brides! Fun in the summer sun!

Twelve heartwarming, sweet novellas linked by a unifying theme.
You'll want to read each one!

BEACH BRIDES SERIES (Jenny)
Twelve friends from the online group, Romantic Hearts Book Club, decide to finally meet in person during a destination Caribbean vacation to beautiful Enchanted Island. While of different ages and stages in life, these ladies have two things in common: 1) they are diehard romantics, and 2) they've been let down by love. As a wildly silly dare during her last night on the island, each heroine decides to stuff a note in a bottle addressed to her "dream hero" and cast it out to sea! Sending a message in a bottle can't be any crazier than online or cell phone dating, or posting personal ads!

And, who knows? One of these mysterious missives might actually lead to love...

Join Meg, Tara, Nina, Clair, Jenny, Lisa, Hope, Kim, Rose, Lily, Faith and Amy, as they embark on the challenge of a lifetime: risking their hearts to accomplish their dreams.

This is Jenny's story....

When a soldier responds to an author's message in a bottle, she can't resist replying, but their online friendship takes a surprising turn when she receives a call that he's been injured and wants to see her.

Meet the Beach Brides!

MEG (Julie Jarnagin)
TARA (Ginny Baird)
NINA (Stacey Joy Netzel)
CLAIR (Grace Greene)
JENNY (Melissa McClone)
LISA (Denise Devine)
HOPE (Aileen Fish)
KIM (Magdalena Scott)
ROSE (Shanna Hatfield)
LILY (Ciara Knight)
FAITH (Helen Scott Taylor)
AMY (Raine English)

PROLOGUE

JENNY'S MESSAGE IN a Bottle...

Dear Bottle Finder:

You have precisely forty-two minutes to complete your mission or life as you know it will end. If you happen to be color blind and can't tell the red wire from the others, just crack open a beer or unwrap a candy bar and enjoy the next forty-one minutes before it's all over.

Oh, wait.

Wrong mission.

Let's try this again...

I'm on a Caribbean vacation with my girlfriends, and we're tossing messages in bottles into the sea in hopes of finding true love. Please understand that alcohol was free flowing when we decided to do this. No, fruity rum drinks with paper umbrellas aren't an excuse, but they were delicious! And who knows? Maybe dream heroes do exist, and ours are out there!

I'd love to say I'm a complete romantic, and that I believe in my heart of hearts whoever's reading this is my soul mate, but I also think we're one EMP away from an ELE. If those acronyms have you heading to Google to do a search, then you likely aren't my other half.

If by some miracle, or alien intervention, you are reading this and think, hey, this could be the woman of my dreams, then your mission is to email me at the address below if you:

- *Are single and male.*
- *Think something strange did happen in Roswell.*
- *Know your name will never be on the FBI's Most-Wanted List.*
- *Aren't allergic to cats or dogs.*
- *Prefer armchair traveling to jet-setting.*

Or...if you're certain I'm not the one for you, but want to let me know where you found the bottle and that you read this message, feel free to email me, too, so I can die of embarrassment.

Cheers,
JH
8675309@...

CHAPTER ONE

Thirteen months later...

AT TWO O'CLOCK in the morning, Jenny Hanford still sat at her desk in the half-lit office on the first floor of her house. Day or night, nothing much happened in Berry Lake, Washington, a small town located north of the Columbia River Gorge. Maybe that was why she'd grown up devouring novels and now wrote books full of intrigue, espionage, and non-stop action.

Jenny stifled a yawn.

Yes, she was tired, but sleep could wait until she finished the draft of her new novel, *Assassin Fever*—the next volume in her bestselling thriller series called the Thorpe Files, which featured spy extraordinaire Ashton Thorpe.

Almost there...

As sights, sounds, and smells swirled through her mind, her fingers flew over the keyboard. The tapping sound became nothing more than white noise. She focused on the screen. Letters turned into words that became sentences and then paragraphs.

Her breath caught in her throat.

Tears stung her eyes.

Oh, Ash. You did it. You saved the world. Again.

With a sigh, she typed her two favorite words in the English language—*The End.* The draft was finished.

Satisfaction flowed through her.

A good feeling considering she'd been certain the story was the worst thing she'd ever written only four days ago. Still not perfect, but the manuscript didn't suck as badly as she'd thought. All she needed was feedback from her editor so she could do revisions. She typed a quick email, attached the file, and then hit send.

Now she could sleep. Well, once her brain slowed down.

If she went to bed now, she wouldn't sleep. The story still looped through her mind. The elation of finishing mixed with the sadness of saying goodbye for now to her favorite character.

Might as well do something productive until she could no longer stay awake.

The number of emails in her inbox made her do a double take. Jenny groaned. She'd been ignoring everything for almost two weeks, but...

8132.

She groaned again.

Don't look at them.

But, of course, she had to.

Jenny deleted as much of the junk as she could. Message notifications from her online book club could wait until tomorrow. They were used to her disappearing to write. When she'd first joined the Romantic Hearts Book Club, she'd been a full-time textbook editor and part-time author. Now she only edited an occasional textbook project—usually as a favor to her former boss—and wrote full time.

So much had changed over the past four years. Her entire life really, though few knew because she'd never made a big deal over writing as Jenna Ford. She wasn't *that* secretive about her pseudonym, but she'd quickly learned too many people only wanted to be *Jenna's* friend. Not Jenny's.

Maybe that was why her closest friends, other than her sister-in-law and some college classmates, were people she'd met virtually. She could just be herself with them. It was easier that way.

She scrolled through her inbox and deleted what she could. The subject line *"Message in Bottle Found"* caught her attention.

She did a double take. "Seriously?"

Over a year ago—thirteen months to be exact—she'd taken a Caribbean vacation on Enchanted Island with eleven other members of her book club. Meeting in person seemed appropriate after being together online for three years.

Boy, was it ever!

Spending face-to-face time with friends, having fun in the sun, and talking about books had been the perfect getaway. Jenny hadn't realized how badly she'd needed a vacation—or how enjoyable it would be to hang out with women from the book world.

Before they returned home, they'd each tossed a message in a bottle into the ocean in hopes of finding true love. They weren't called the Romantic Hearts for nothing. Surprisingly, a few had met their dream heroes after they received replies and were now married.

Not Jenny.

She'd gone into the bottle toss with zero expectations. Oh, she'd hoped it might work out, but deep in her heart of hearts, she had a feeling it wouldn't. She might write fiction, but her life was no storybook. Her romantic past read more like a comedy—a dark one. She'd assumed a tanker or cargo ship would run over her bottle and the note would never be read. But now…

Jenny tapped on the subject line.

Message in Bottle Found
DOR2008@…
To: Jenny <8675309@…>

Message received, Jenny. I assume that's your name. 867-5309 is one of my mom's favorite songs.

Bottle found on a beach in Key West.

An asteroid has a better chance of causing an ELE than an EMP. Just sayin'.

Roswell, seriously? You should be more embarrassed about that than someone reading your message in a bottle. Guess you're a Bigfoot believer, too.

DOR

P.S. I am single and male, but not in the market for a soul mate. Hope you've found your true love.

Well, her bottle had at least reached an unmarried guy. What were the odds of that?

She laughed at his last line.

Jenny hadn't found her one true love, but that was okay. She had room for only one man in her life.

Yep, good old Ashton Thorpe.

He might only live in her mind and on the pages of her novels, but he was the ultimate book boyfriend—the kind of guy men aspired to be. Her series that featured him had made more money than she'd ever imagined having, and Ash would soon grace the big screen in what the producers hoped would be a successful movie franchise.

He was made for that kind of stardom... if the actor slated to play Ash could pull off his combination of courage, daring, and hotness. The right amount of swagger wouldn't hurt, either.

Larger than life was the only way to describe Ash. Perfect was another. Make believe, yes, but no guy she'd dated could compete. Although... she hadn't given up hope one would someday.

Jenny read the message again. The fact DOR knew the song she used for her email address impressed her. That the bottle reached Key West didn't surprise her given the currents and the amount of time that had passed. The Roswell and Bigfoot comments brought a much-needed smile to her tired face.

Yawning, she typed off a quick reply. The cursor

hovered over the send button.

Another yawn.

In the morning, Jenny would likely regret she'd responded, but she was too tired to care now. She hit send.

****

Army Sergeant Darragh, aka Dare, O'Rourke needed a shower and a nap, not necessarily in that order, but both would have to wait until after the debriefing. As he sat on a bench waiting for the rest of his squad to arrive, he pulled out his cell phone. His mom and his three sisters had texted, but nothing urgent.

Staff Sergeant Mitch Hamilton lumbered up and sat next to Dare. They'd deployed together numerous times. Hamilton was a couple of years older and an excellent leader, one who knew when to get in a soldier's face or act like a big brother.

Yep, usually, he was in Dare's face.

Hamilton stretched out his long, dust-covered legs. "Love training at the range for a few days, but I'm going to enjoy having a long weekend off. I hope Lizzy doesn't hand me a honey-do list the minute I walk through the door."

"Given she does every weekend you are home, I'd say rest up now, Sergeant."

"You're right." Hamilton laughed. "Any plans, O'Rourke?"

"Sleep and more sleep." Dare clicked on his email app. He leaned forward to take a closer look at the screen. "No way."

"Everything okay?" Hamilton asked.

"Yeah." Dare stared at the email from Jenny. "Just got an email from someone."

"A woman?"

He half-laughed. "I think she's a woman."

"Whoa." Hamilton's visible concern made Dare straighten. "Back up, O'Rourke. You think? You don't know?"

"I..." Might as well start at the beginning. "When I was on leave in the Florida Keys, I found a message in a bottle. There was an email address on it. The person wanted to know where the bottle was found, so I wrote back. This is her reply."

"Catfish."

"Maybe." Dare thought about that reality show. Many people had been strung along by an online scammer pretending to be someone they weren't. Although, he *had* made it clear he wasn't looking for romance. "But she had no idea who would find the bottle or if they'd respond. She probably replied because she was lonely."

Weren't most people? Even though Dare was surrounded by amazing guys—his brothers-in-arms who would risk their lives for him—he was lonely at times.

"If she replied with a marriage proposal or nude pic, she's catfishing," Hamilton said.

If she had, Dare was hitting the delete key. Call him old-fashioned, but no.

"Guess we'll find out." He opened the email.

Re: Message in Bottle Found

Jenny <8675309@...>
To: DOR2008@...

You deduced the song reference correctly, however...

Jenny suffered only mild embarrassment, rather than death, after realizing someone read her message in the bottle. That led her to go hiking in the woods nearby. No one has heard from her since. Large footprints and splotches of dark, smelly fur were found at her last-known location.

Sasquatch lives. Possible soul mate? Let's hope so for

Jenny's sake.

P.S. Embarrassed by Roswell? Never. Just because you haven't seen a UFO doesn't mean they don't exist.

P.P.S. I haven't seen a UFO myself, but the documentaries on Roswell are fascinating. Watch one if you get the chance. It happened!

Dare laughed. No marriage proposal or nude pic, but Jenny was funny. A little off the wall, but he'd known that from her bottle message.

Hamilton read the email when Dare tilted the phone toward him. "Good sense of humor. Sounds smart. A little geeky. I think you've found yourself a girl. Write her back."

"I have no idea who she is or if she's even real. Why would I keep this going?"

Hamilton looked around as if to see if anyone was near. No one stood close enough to overhear. "Because this is the biggest smile I've seen on your face in over a year. It's time you moved on, Dare."

That was the first time he'd heard Hamilton use his nickname in months. Not since Mitch had been promoted to staff sergeant.

"I've moved on," Dare said.

"Really?"

The disbelief in Hamilton's voice made Dare bristle. What could he say?

There hadn't been much for him to smile about. A year and a half ago, he'd discovered his girlfriend, Kayla, was cheating on him with his best friend, Brock. Dare had been planning to propose. Instead, his trust had been betrayed by the two people closest to him in the worst possible way. At least Brock had transferred to a different company. Seeing him every day would have sucked.

Dare dragged the toe of his boot across the asphalt. "Yes."

"When was your last date, O'Rourke?"

He shrugged. That wasn't an answer, but the truth would only give Hamilton more ammunition.

A corner of the staff sergeant's mouth lifted. "That long ago, huh?"

Dare nodded once. He hadn't felt like meeting women after what happened with Kayla and Brock. Not wanting to be hurt again had been his priority.

"I've been thinking about dating," Dare finally said.

"Maybe this Jenny person is a way to get in the game and put yourself out there."

Dare drank a swig of water.

"What have you got to lose?" Hamilton asked.

"Money and my identity if she, or he, is a scammer."

Hamilton cursed. "You're a United States Army Ranger, O'Rourke. You'd better be smarter than that."

"I am." Granted, he'd been clueless about what Kayla had been doing with Brock or maybe Dare just hadn't wanted to see.

"Then reply." Hamilton's tone challenged Dare the same way it had in the past, often in a faraway land on a different continent. "You know you want to."

Maybe Dare did. He typed a quick email.

"Send it," Hamilton ordered.

"You can't tell me what to do in my personal life."

"I can, and I did." Hamilton laughed. "Relax, O'Rourke. I'm only doing this because it's for your own good."

Dare hesitated. Keeping the email exchange going made no sense. "This is a bad idea."

"When have you let that stop you before, O'Rourke?"

They didn't call him Dare for nothing. "Never."

He didn't know why he was putting so much thought into this. It was just an email. No big deal. He'd probably never hear from Jenny again.

Dare hit send. "Done."

CHAPTER TWO

JENNY SAT ON the big, overstuffed reading chair in the corner of her office. It was more comfortable working on revisions on her laptop here than at her desk. Her back couldn't take much more sitting there.

She reread part of her editor's notes on *Assassin Fever*. Rewriting a short scene had taken her the entire morning. This didn't bode well for the rest of the manuscript. Still, making the story better was worth the work.

Her stomach growled.

She needed food—not the M&M's peanut or plain variety. Maybe after she rewrote another scene.

Footsteps sounded on the hardwood floor. "Ready for lunch?"

The sound of her sister-in-law's voice brought a smile. Jenny should have known Missy would come to her rescue. "Yes, because I'm starving."

"Not enough to stop writing and feed yourself." Missy Hanford carried a tray of food. As she walked, her auburn-colored ponytail bounced. "Which is why you have me around."

The smells made Jenny's mouth water. "I don't know what I'd do without you."

"Same, though I have enough sense to eat more than peanut M&M's for breakfast. Plus, enough self-control I can avoid the internet without having to ask someone else to turn off the router when I need to get something done."

Missy and Rob, Jenny's little brother, had known each other their entire lives, became boyfriend and girlfriend in middle school, and married at eighteen after Rob joined the United States Marines. Their dreams of having a house full of kids and a happily ever after ended when an IED in Afghanistan killed Rob. He'd been twenty-three.

"I'm a writer. I have no sense. Most days, I don't even get out of my pajamas," Jenny admitted. "If I turn off the Wi-Fi, I know I can turn it on, but I don't even know where the router is."

"Whatever gets the book finished." Missy set the tray on top of the desk, which was covered with marked-up pieces of paper. "I don't mind turning the router on and off, but you should know where it is. I'm not always here."

Six years had passed since Rob's death, and not a day went by that Jenny didn't think about him. Missy continued to struggle with her grief. If not for the two cats she and Rob had adopted before that fateful deployment, Missy might have given up, but her good days now outnumbered the bad ones. Although she hadn't shown any interest in dating or men in general.

"I don't mind waiting for you to get home," Jenny said.

Rob had asked her to watch out for his wife before he deployed, and Jenny had. After her first Thorpe Files novel hit it big, she'd wanted to move out of her tiny apartment and buy a house. One of the selling points of this place had been a two-bedroom separate guesthouse where Missy could live. They had privacy, but could still look out for each other. The arrangement had worked out well, especially after Missy became Jenny's personal assistant. She knew it was what Rob would have wanted.

"Chicken satay, spring rolls, wontons, yellow curry, shrimp pad thai, and white rice. I ordered extra so there would be leftovers." Missy drew her eyebrows together in an exaggerated expression. "You do know how to use a microwave, right, or should I leave instructions for that?"

"Ha-ha."

"Don't laugh," Missy said. "I'm going to be working longer shifts this week at the cupcake shop.

The chemo is hitting Elise hard. I offered to take on more hours so she didn't have to keep juggling work schedules. Bad timing with your revisions, I know. Sorry."

"It's not a problem. You're the best assistant an author could ask for, and that's a nice thing to do for your boss." Missy had worked at the same cupcake shop since she was fifteen. She didn't need the money as much as she liked the familiarity and staying busy. "Elise needs more help than I do."

"Yeah, right." With a laugh, Missy fixed herself a plate. "Come over here and eat before you pass out. Did you sleep last night?"

"A couple of hours." The smells called to Jenny. Eating would give her the energy to keep revising. "I couldn't stop thinking about what changes the manuscript needed, so I decided to make some of them."

As Jenny reached for the top of her screen, she noticed an email in her inbox. She'd been obsessive about not letting her emails get out of control again. Maybe she could delete it without reading. She clicked on the postage-stamp icon on the bottom of her screen.

The message's subject line sent her pulse racing. DOR had replied.

Re: Re: Message in Bottle Found
DOR2008@...
To: Jenny <8675309@...>

Pic or it never happened.

Short and sweet, but the words made her smile.

"What are you looking at?" Missy asked.

"An email."

Jenny had told Missy about tossing a message in a bottle when she got home from vacation, but not about someone finding it, emailing, and her replying. Her sister-in-law might freak over Jenny doing something so out of character. Maybe that was why receiving a reply gave Jenny a little thrill.

Her stomach grumbled.

Missy motioned her over. "You need to eat."

"I'm coming." Jenny wanted to reply, but she needed something before she could do that. She closed her computer and joined her sister-in-law at the desk. Lunch looked as tasty as it smelled. "How hard would it be to find a decent picture of Bigfoot?"

"Given Berry Lake is Bigfoot central, not hard."

"See if you can find one that doesn't look too fake."

"Do I want to know why you need this?" Missy

asked.

Grinning, Jenny filled a plate. "Probably not."

****

Re: Re: Re: *Message in Bottle Found*
Jenny <8675309@...>
To: DOR2008@...

Jenny is trapped in Bigfoot's lair. He's so tall. Pic attached.

****

Re: Re: Re: Re: Message in Bottle
DOR2008@...
To: Jenny <8675309@...>

Did you think I'd fall for a photo put together with lousy photo-editing skills? If that blurry person in the background is you, you could be three feet tall or six. The hairy guy is bigger, but there's no way to determine heights.

Show me the real Bigfoot and include scale.

****

Pics

Jenny <8675309@...>
To: DOR2008@...

I'm trying to escape from Bigfoot's lair, and you're worried about scale?

P.S. I'm neither of those heights. I fall in between.

****

Standing in the hallway outside the command's offices, Dare stared at the email he'd forwarded to Jenny that had been returned to his inbox with a bunch of nonsensical numbers and letters. Her address was correct. He'd been using that one for days. Yet, he'd received an undeliverable message from mailer-daemon.

It didn't make sense.

Their exchanges had been fun. Nothing flirty or weird. But he liked hearing from her.

Maybe her inbox was full. That happened sometimes, right?

Dare would try again. He hoped it would go through.

****

The router had been turned off for over a week, but that allowed Jenny to work on the revisions without distractions. She'd even finished a day early since it was still ten minutes to midnight.

Sitting at her desk, she attached the *Assassin Fever* manuscript and clicked send. The swooshing sound of the email shooting across the internet brought a palpable relief.

Time to celebrate.

She unwrapped a candy bar.

The story had clicked during revisions, and she couldn't be happier with the result. She hoped readers agreed.

Ash Thorpe had saved the day—well, mankind— once again, but in the process, he'd lost another love. Someday, he'd get a happily ever after. No more dodging bullets, defusing bombs, and capturing terrorists and assorted bad guys. Just smiles, laughter, and love.

The forever, true-love kind.

Most likely before she got hers.

She bit into the candy bar. The combination of caramel, peanuts, and chocolate was one of her favorites.

The little postage stamp at the bottom of her screen displayed the number 3413. That wasn't as many emails that had accumulated the last time she'd been on deadline, but Missy had warned her the email provider had experienced an outage at some point. That meant she would have had more if that hadn't happened.

Might as well see what she'd missed. Jenny opened her inbox and scrolled through the emails.

Delete. Delete. Flag to reply later. Delete. Forward to Missy. Flag. Delete.

This wasn't too bad. She kept going. Maybe if she could get through a few hundred tonight...

Oh. Wow.

She leaned closer to the screen. The bottle guy had replied two days ago. She clicked on the email.

Re: Fwd: Search for Bigfoot Special

DOR2008@...

To: Jenny <8675309@...>

Are you okay?

Not a stalker or weird guy, but I haven't heard from you. Please reply when you get the chance.

Dare

Aww. He—*Dare*—sounded worried. That was

sweet, as was how he didn't want her to think he was strange. If he were a sociopath, she doubted he'd have written the words stalker and weird in his email.

Jenny reread his message. She felt as if she were missing something. There had to be another email she hadn't seen yet. She scrolled through her inbox until she found it.

Fwd: Search for Bigfoot Special
DOR2008@...
To: Jenny <8675309@...>

Jenny,

I emailed you about an upcoming Bigfoot show I thought you might want to watch, but the email was returned undeliverable. Trying again.

P.S. Keep it Squatchy.

The Squatchy line made her smile. Missy had given her a baseball cap with those words on it for Christmas. Guess Dare wasn't as anti-Bigfoot as he appeared. Maybe there was hope for Roswell.

Jenny laughed. Something she never expected to be doing post-deadline and exhausted.

"Thanks, Dare."

Whoever the guy was, he seemed nice. Thoughtful.

Her face felt warm, and her heart was full.

Missy worried about her, but she was family. Jenny liked the thought of someone else caring what happened to her, even though he was a total stranger.

Her candy bar was waiting, but she would let Dare know she was okay first. That was the least she could do for the bottle guy.

****

Waking up to reveille would be more welcome than the blaring buzz, buzz, buzz of the phone alarm. Dare hit the off button, but he didn't get out of bed. Thoughts about Jenny had kept him up late last night. Again. He needed more sleep.

Stupid.

For all he knew, Jenny didn't exist. She could be a scammer. Not replying was probably part of her game plan to pull him in.

It was working.

He was concerned something had happened to her.

Weird.

Getting worked up and worried over a person he'd

never met was crazy. If anything, those feelings showed Dare how lonely he was. Maybe Hamilton was right—it was time to start dating again.

Something casual and fun.

That might be nice.

He rubbed his face, the stubble rough against his fingers.

Going out would be better than sitting at home waiting for a reply from a stranger. Okay, he wasn't *that* bad, but the next time the guys were off to the bar, he would go with them.

Dare picked up his phone to read his texts. A joke from a friend. A link to a news article from another. He would read that when he was more awake. He checked his email. Blinked. Bolted upright.

Jenny.

Finally.

Re: Re: Fwd: Search for Bigfoot Special

Jenny <8675309@...>

To: Dare <DOR2008@...>

Hey, Dare. I'm okay. Sorry I missed the special. I'll see if I can find it streaming somewhere. Made it out of Bigfoot's lair. He's too smelly for me. I wasn't hairy enough for him. Guess true love will have to wait.

Dare is a cool name, btw. Hope all is well with you!

Jenny

P.S. Thanks for the concern. There was a glitch with my email provider, so I didn't get emails for a day or two. Not that I was online to read them. Had a big project due. Stayed offline to finish. Sorry.

P.P.S. If my email fails again or if texting is easier, you can reach me at 360-555-0147.

Dare released the breath he hadn't realized he was holding. Jenny was not only okay, but she'd also given him her phone number. A win-win.

He added her number to his contacts. No last name, but that was okay. The less she told him about herself, the less he'd need to share about his life. Jenny could still be a scammer—though nothing she'd done made him think that—but he liked having another way to contact her.

He also preferred texting to email. His phone was right here.

Might as well send a message now...

CHAPTER THREE

Dare: *It's Dare. Thanks for the number. Texting is easier. Bigfoot's loss.*

Jenny: *Aw, thanks. You're up early. Unless you're on the East Coast. The sun is still asleep here.*

Dare: *Where's here? I'm in Georgia.*

Jenny: *Washington.*

That meant a three-hour time difference. It was still the middle of the night where she lived.

Dare: *Sorry I woke you.*

Jenny: *I was awake. My sleep pattern is completely off due to working crazy hours to finish my project.*

Dare: *That happens to me. Exhausted, need to sleep, but can't.*

Jenny: *Exactly. I can't shut off my brain.*

Dare: *I was the same way last night.*

Jenny: *Everything okay?*

Dare: *Yes. Today's looking much better.*

Jenny: *Good. I should try to sleep or I'll be a zombie all day.*

Dare: *Sleep well.*

Jenny: *TTYL.*

Jenny could count on him talking to her later.

With a big smile on his face, Dare leaned against his pillow and reread her texts.

****

After two weeks of texting with Dare, Jenny decided the time had come to tell her book club that she'd heard back from the person who found her message in the bottle. She wasn't sure why she'd kept that a secret when she looked forward to hearing from him. The exchanges were mostly silly, but she liked waking up to his texts.

Sitting on the living room couch, she typed a message to tell her friends what she knew about Dare—he lived in Georgia and found her bottle on a beach in Key West—and that their exchanges were friendly, not flirty.

Which was fine with her.

So far, five of the book club members had heard

from their bottle finders. Not quite half, but that was a better percentage than Jenny had expected.

Meg's message had led to her being invited on the reality TV show *One True Love*. She'd ended up falling in love with the producer, not one of the contestants. Jenny doubted anyone would be able to top that. She sure wouldn't.

Dare's first email about him not being in the market for a soul mate or wanting to find true love had been a clear warning, and that was good. It made writing to him easier.

No pressure. No reason to read anything into what he wrote.

Her message in a bottle might not have brought her a happily ever after, but she'd made a new friend. One whose emails and texts brought a smile to her face and didn't make her feel so isolated and lonely when she spent so much of her time by herself.

She closed her laptop and walked into the kitchen. Missy was unloading the dishwasher. She was working her regular shift at the cupcake shop now that Elise was feeling better.

"We have a housekeeper to do that," Jenny said.

"She doesn't come every day, and I want to bake cookies. There's stuff I need in here." Missy wore colorful paw-print leggings and an oversized T-shirt with *Semper Fi* written across the front. "We're going to celebrate!"

"What are we celebrating? Did another cat from the rescue get adopted?"

"No, but your new bookmarks arrived. They're gorgeous." She pointed to a small cardboard box on the counter. "And while I was at the post office picking them up, I bumped into Josh Cooper. He's been meaning to call you. Mentioned something about you two getting together."

"I..." Words failed Jenny.

Josh had been her high school crush. Who was she kidding? He'd been every girl's fantasy.

Smart, athletic, hot.

"What's he doing in town?" she asked. "I thought he was a big-time sports announcer."

"He is. Football, I think, but he bought a house not too far from here. Said he needed a home base. Since he owns a plane, he can easily fly to the Portland airport if he can't get to a game directly."

"A plane, huh? Moving home should be good for him."

"And you." Missy pulled out a measuring cup and mixing bowl from the dishwasher. "You can finally go out with your dream guy."

"My dream guy when I was a teenager." That was

well over a decade ago. "Josh isn't going to ask me on a date. He probably wants to have an old classmate stroke his ego."

"Or another appendage." Missy grinned.

Jenny shook her head.

"What? He's still attractive, and you had a thing for him once. That's why I gave him your number. You need to get out more."

"I get out as much as you."

She shot Jenny a no-you-don't look. "I have two jobs—one at the cupcake shop and one with you—and I volunteer at the cat rescue."

"I work from home."

"Exactly. Going out with Josh will be good for you."

"I get out to do book signings or writer workshops and events."

"Not enough, especially when those are work related. You're thirty-one. Pretty and successful. You should be dating, partying, and having the time of your life."

"I'm happiest staying at home and writing. I can't help it. I'm boring."

Missy tsked. "What am I going to do with you?"

"Keep feeding me, sending my reader newsletter to fans, and staying on top of my social media."

"You know I will, but please say yes when Josh calls. He could be the one for you."

"He just wants to go out with Jenna Ford."

Guys hit on Jenna Ford a hundred times more than Jenny Hanford. The reason was money. Jenna Ford had bank.

Been there, done that, gave back the ring two weeks before the wedding.

Three years ago, she'd discovered her then-fiancé, Grant, had racked up six-figures worth of gambling debt. He'd claimed to have gone to rehab to help his addiction. She'd had no reason to doubt him, but friends had suggested she postpone the wedding to give Grant time to pay off the debt so she wouldn't have to. It had sounded like a smart idea to Jenny. Except Grant hadn't wanted to wait. He'd wanted to get married as they'd planned.

Jenny was willing, but she decided to speak to her CPA and her attorney first. Both recommended she have Grant sign a prenuptial agreement so her assets would not be used to pay off his debt. Her lawyer had also added verbiage so that Grant gave up his rights to her intellectual properties, aka books.

Grant wouldn't sign it. During a tantrum worthy of a two-year-old, he'd claimed to have only proposed because she was Jenna Ford and rich. He'd said no man would ever be interested in Jenny Hanford.

She'd thrown the engagement ring at him. Not her finest moment, but his words had decimated her self-confidence. She'd been devastated. Not because she canceled the wedding—that was just collateral damage—but from being viewed as an easy mark to be taken advantage of by a handsome, money-hungry charmer. She'd lost faith that decent men existed. Or if they did, in her ability to find them.

"Josh didn't mention Jenna." The disapproval in Missy's eyes stung. "He called you Jenny."

Jenny lifted her chin. "Don't give me that look. Remember Grant?"

"Grant was a taker. A total loser looking for a quick payout. Josh knew you before Jenna."

"And he's never said a word to me. Not during high school. Or when we were in college and came home during the holidays."

Now he wanted to get together? Call her paranoid, but she hoped Josh didn't call.

****

Jenny: *Hope you are doing well today.*
Dare: *What's wrong?*
Jenny: *What do you mean?*

Dare: *Something's up.*

Jenny: *Why do you think that?*

Dare: *You always start out with something more off the wall.*

Jenny: *You know me that well already?*

Dare: *Am I wrong?*

Jenny: *No.*

Dare: *Spill.*

Jenny: *I got asked out.*

Dare: *By?*

Jenny: *A guy I knew in high school. He moved back to town and wants to get together for coffee.*

Dare: *Coffee sounds like a good first date.*

Jenny: *Yes, but I don't want to go.*

Dare: *Why not?*

Jenny: *The guy is allergic to cats. That's a deal breaker for me.*

Dare: *How many cats do you have?*

Jenny: *None.*

Dare: *Then why is it a deal breaker?*

Jenny: *What if I want a cat (or a dog) in the future, but couldn't get one due to someone else's allergies? So, yes, a deal breaker. And why it was on my list.*

Dare: *List?*

Jenny: *Message-in-the-bottle list.*

Dare: *Oh, yeah. But think about this for a minute. You'd really walk away from the hypothetically perfect guy for a cat (or dog) you may or may not even want in the future?*

Jenny: *I never said he was perfect. But yes, because that's not all.*

Dare: *What?*

Jenny: *He doesn't believe in aliens or Bigfoot.*

Dare: *You asked?*

Jenny: *Sort of.*

Dare: *Not much you can do about allergies, but differences can be overcome if you care enough.*

Jenny: *Speaking from experience?*

Dare: *Yes, though she liked my best friend better than me. Ended up with two exes by the time that was over.*

Jenny: *Ouch. That had to hurt.*

Dare: *Yep.*

Jenny: *You're better off without people like that in your life. Though, maybe the differences between you were more the deal-breaker kind.*

Dare: *You may be right, but that shouldn't stop you from saying yes to coffee.*

Jenny: *You think so?*

Dare: *Could be fun.*

Jenny: *I guess.*

Dare: *But you need to be careful. Drive yourself. A coffee house is a public place, so that's good. Be sure to let a friend know your plans.*

Jenny: *Big brother, uncle, or dad?*

Dare: *Three sisters. Let me know what you decide.*

Two days later...

Jenny: *I said yes.*

Dare: *And?*

Jenny: *I didn't think meeting for coffee could be so horrible. I was wrong.*

Dare: *You okay?*

Jenny: *Yes. I owe you a thank you.*

Dare: *Why?*

Jenny: *I followed your instructions. You saved me from things being much worse.*

Dare: *What happened?*

Jenny: *He'd been drinking before he arrived, called me the wrong name the entire time, put a picture of us on Instagram as if we were a couple, and then asked if I wanted to go to his place to have sex.*

Dare: *What—are you joking?*

Jenny: *I wish I were kidding. I have a feeling his*

drinking might be one of the reasons he's moving back here. I hope he gets the help he needs, but lesson learned. I'm going to stick to my list in the future.

Dare: *The guy's a loser. The list rules from now on.*

Jenny: *Yes!*

Dare: *You might want to take a self-defense class. Just in case.*

Jenny: *I might.*

Dare: *Do and shake this off. You gave it a shot. That's what matters. It's not your fault the guy is a jerk and a drunk.*

Jenny: *Thanks. Any hot dates for you?*

Dare: *Not lately. Married to the job. Big trip coming up.*

Jenny: *Work won't seem as important when you meet the right person. At least, that's what my friends tell me.*

Dare: *These wouldn't be the same friends who tossed bottles into the sea with you?*

Jenny: *Yes, they would be. A few have even fallen in love and gotten married to the guys who found their bottles.*

Dare: *Wow. That's great.*

Jenny: *Very happy for them.*

Dare: *But poor you ended up with me.*

Jenny: *Not poor me. I have a new friend.*

Dare: *Hope this doesn't sound weird, but I'm glad I found your bottle.*

Jenny: *Not weird, and so am I.*

****

Gear packed and ready to go before sunrise, Dare sat on the floor with his back against the wall as rangers from his company gathered. He tried to shut out the conversations around him. He needed to write Jenny.

Just thinking her name made him smile.

They'd been texting almost every day, depending on what he had going on with the pre-deployment workup, and he wanted to tell her he was leaving on his "big trip." Not a lie. A deployment *was* a big trip.

He hadn't known what else to tell her. They hadn't shared much personal information. He had no idea what she did for a living, where in Washington she lived, or how old she was. His curiosity grew by the day, but there was no rush in finding out more about her. He hoped she was careful if she got asked out again and remembered what he'd told her.

Dare typed an email. He had more to say than would work via text. He didn't want Jenny to think he disappeared on her if he couldn't get online.

"Wheels up at zero six thirty, O'Rourke," Hamilton barked. "Is your squad ready?"

Dare's guys had been ready three days ago. "Yes, Sergeant."

"Don't you have something else to do?"

"Just need to send an email first."

"To your girl? Jenny?"

Dare nodded. He liked the idea of Jenny being his girl.

A corner of Hamilton's mouth lifted into a smirk. "Carry on, O'Rourke, but make it quick. I'm counting on you to ensure a smooth departure."

CHAPTER FOUR

OUT OF CONTACT
Dare <DOR2008@...>
To: Jenny <8675309@j...>

Jenny,

Remember how I mentioned a big trip with work? I'm leaving today. Not sure about cell coverage where we're going. Spotty Wi-Fi for sure. I might not be able to respond for a while, but I'll be in touch when I can. Until then, take Bigfoot repellent with you when you hike. Can't have you trapped in his lair again. And be careful when you go out on dates. Please remember the precautions I told you.

Take care,
Dare

****

Re: Out of Contact

Jenny <8675309@...>
To: Dare <DOR2008@...>

Dare,

Thanks for letting me know. I hope your trip goes well. Safe travels! Repellent is in my purse. Might come in handy in other situations. No more dates planned, however. The message-in-the-bottle list is good at weeding people out. If someone does meet the requirements, I will be careful and remember your precautions. Promise!

Thanks,
Jenny

****

Been a while
Dare <DOR2008@...>
To: Jenny <8675309@...>

Hey, Jenny,

Sorry to be out of touch for so long. Okay, two weeks isn't that long, but it feels like forever. It's been crazy busy here. I had a free minute and an internet connection, so I wanted to say hi and that I was thinking about you.

That's probably weird when I know nothing about you except your first name and the state where you live, but I miss our texting. Can't wait to get home so we can do that again. Unless, of course, you're dating someone and he's the jealous type. Totally would understand if that's the case. If you were my girl, I wouldn't want you texting some random dude. If you're not with someone, I hope you haven't had to use the repellent!

As for life here, it's not bad. Food sucks, and I'd love a burger, fries, and chocolate milkshake right now, but things could be worse. We're getting the job done, and that's what matters.

Take care,
Dare

P.S. Dare is a nickname for Darragh. A family name. My great-grandfather. Don't think I ever told you that.
P.P.S. I was outside last night and looked up at the

sky. It was a clear night and breathtaking. I thought of you and wondered if you had the same view. I know some parts of Washington get a lot of rain, but I hope it wasn't cloudy where you live.

****

Re: Been a while

Jenny <8675309@...>

To: Dare <DOR2008@...>

Hey, Dare,

Great to hear from you. I know business trips can be insane so not surprised you're busy.

No burgers where you are? In your honor, I ate the meal you've been wanting, and it was delicious. Especially the shake, but how can you go wrong when chocolate is involved? The hamburger was grilled just right, slightly juicy but not too much pink (not a fan of rare), and the French fries were waffle-cut with seasoned salt. Yum!

And not weird. I've been thinking about you, too, even though I only know your first name and that you live in Georgia. My real name is Jennifer, in case you hadn't guessed, but Jenny fits me better, and is what everyone calls me.

But this might be weird. I was so happy when I saw your email in my inbox today. It put a big smile on my face. Not that I was frowning or sad, just tired and a little overwhelmed with work.

No dates, but that's okay. I've had a lot to do, and my sister-in-law's having a rougher time than usual. My brother died six years ago, and the anniversary of his death was last week. She's stronger than she realizes, but they got married a week after high school graduation, and he was her world. I keep telling her there is no time frame for grief. I just wish there was something else I could say to make things better.

She's into animal rescue, and I help her sometimes. The other night, we were out until two in the morning with her rescue group trapping feral cats. They have a program where a vet will neuter or spay and give shots before the rescue releases the cats back where they were found.

I so wish I could see your sky. I love stargazing, but

even though it's summer, the nights have been overcast. I'll keep trying. The clouds can't stay out forever.

Well, I guess that's all for now. Hope you're managing to have some fun!

Jenny

P.S. Repellant remains unused. Very pleased about that.

P.P.S. Any chance you've had time to date while on the road? I went on mine, so it's your turn.

****

Re: Re: Been a while
Dare <DOR2008@...>
To: Jenny <8675309@...>

Jenny,

Great to hear from you! I figured your name was Jennifer. I like Jenny.
Thanks for eating in my honor. I have another meal

mission for you should you choose to accept it:

Corn dog, tater tots, and soda (no diet, full-on sugar).

Glad I could put a smile on your face. Your email did the same for me. Guess I was smiling more than usual because I got some ribbing from the guys I work with. I told them they're jealous. I probably shouldn't have said that. When I told them we're just friends, no one believed me.

I'm sorry about your brother. I've lost a few friends, and it sucks. Your sister-in-law is lucky to have someone like you. Not sure it'll help, but the wife of a good friend who died is now remarried with a baby on the way. She was in a dark place for a while, but then she realized her husband wouldn't have wanted her to stop living (and she wouldn't have wanted that if the situation had been reversed). She knows he would want her to live the life they'd planned and make their dreams come true. So that's what she did. I didn't want to like the guy she married, but I must admit, he's good for her. Totally different from my friend, but that's what she needed.

Animal rescue in the dead of the night, huh? Good

work and glad you were with a group, but be careful when you're out late in the dark. Please don't do that alone or with just your sister-in-law. Not to harp on this, but you really should take a self-defense class. Better safe than sorry.

Sounds like you have enough going on not to be dating. That makes two of us.

Have the clouds parted so you can see the starry night? I hope so, but if not, I'm watching the skies for both of us. I took a few pictures I'll share when I'm home. Sorry, no UFOs that I could see, but I keep looking for them. There's a particularly bright star (had to make sure it wasn't a planet) that I call Jenny after you. So beautiful. I'll try to figure out the real name and location so you can look for it.

Not much else is going on. Ready to go home, but not sure when that will be. More work to do.

Be safe,
Dare

****

Mission Accomplished

Jenny <8675309@...>
To: Dare <DOR2008@...>

Sorry for your friends' ribbing, but let them believe what they want. We know the truth! BFFs! And in case that's a new acronym for you, it stands for Bottle Friends Forever!

I don't know when I last ate a corn dog (maybe a fair when I was a teenager?) but meal mission #2 is completed. I'm not a fan of soda (diet or regular), but I suffered through the sweetness for you. Happy to take on another meal mission should you desire.

I shared with my sister-in-law what you told me about your friend's wife, and Missy got really quiet. She said to tell you thanks. I don't know if it'll make a difference, but she needs to hear stuff like that from people other than me. Thank you! I hope someday she can remarry like your friend's wife. Though at this point, going out on a date would be a huge step for Missy. She was also very happy I have a new friend. She thinks I don't get out enough, but what can I say? I'm a homebody.

I wish I could see the Jenny star. Thanks for telling

me about it. I'd love to know what star it really is. The clouds cleared for a brief time last night. I stood on my patio bundled in a blanket. Lots of stars, but the best part was imagining you looking up at the sky, too.

I hope you're home soon.

Thinking about you,
Jenny

****

Re: Mission Accomplished

Dare <DOR2008@...>
To: Jenny <8675309@...>

I've never had a BFF. Glad my first one is you! My team still thinks there's more going on than friendship, so I smile and nod when they ask for details.

Looking at the sky each night and knowing you're doing the same makes me feel like I'm not so far away from home. It's a good feeling, just what I need. Thanks.

The Jenny star seems to be even brighter than before. I'm still trying to figure out the official information. I may have to make a wish that I can get that for you.

I hope Missy is doing better this week. You're a great sister-in-law to care so much about her. It's a good sign she listened even if she was only humoring you. Stuff will sink in eventually—probably already has—but as you wrote, grief doesn't have a time frame. When I'm home, I'll reach out to my friend's widow. She might have more ideas.

Nothing wrong with being a homebody. After a while, the bars and clubs all look the same.

No meal mission for you, but I'd love if you could go on a dessert one—I'd like a warm chocolate brownie, two scoops of vanilla ice cream, hot fudge, whipped cream, and a cherry on top. Make that two cherries. One for each of us.

I'm out of time, so I'll sign off. Can't wait to hear from you. Your emails are keeping me going, Jenny. If that's weird, I don't care.
Your BFF,
Dare

****

Re: Re: Mission Accomplished

Jenny <8675309@...>

To: Dare <DOR2008@...>

Hey, BFF!

Guess what? I made a wish on a star, too. I can't tell you the wish, but I hope yours and mine both come true. There's no rush on getting the star info. It might be fun figuring that out together when you get home. Any word when that will be?

The dessert mission was completed. A total success. Excellent choice, but totally decadent. The calories went straight to my hips. Not that I minded because it was that delicious.

I really could use a BFF, especially if you can be a voice of reason because the logical side of my brain has gone missing. Missy is fostering a litter of kittens. They are the cutest things ever. Tiny and a ton of work. We're bottle feeding them around the clock. They make these little mews and are so soft and cuddly. They fall asleep on you. My heart melts every time I'm around them.

Please tell me I don't need to adopt a kitten. They are adorable, yes, but would be a huge responsibility. One I'm not sure I'm ready for. Did you know there's a cat that is thirty-one years old? That's the same age as me!

Missy says I'm overthinking this, but I've had this plan, sort of a life plan, for a while. It's old-fashioned, but I don't think there's anything wrong with doing things like my parents or grandparents did (i.e. fall in love, get married, have kids, adopt a pet or two in that order). That makes logical sense to me. But what happens if I do stuff out of order? If I adopt a kitten, will it mess up everything else? I'm not the spontaneous type, but I fear one of those cute bundles of fur will be my downfall.

Not much else is going on other than the kittens and work. I'm going to head outside in a few minutes to look at the stars and will be thinking of you doing the same.

Wishing you were here,

Jenny

P.S. That wasn't my wish on a star. Just in case you thought I'd let it slip.

CHAPTER FIVE

JENNY KNEELED IN her backyard. The ground beneath her knees was rock hard. Sweat dotted her hairline beneath her wide-brimmed hat and ran down her neck. She wiped her face with her gardening glove. A good thing she'd slathered on sunscreen or she'd be getting sunburned.

The temperature was a scorcher on this August day. She glanced at Missy. "It's hot, but it feels good to be outside."

"That's the spirit." Missy dug holes to plant pink impatiens. She'd said the yard needed more color, left the house, and returned with flats of flowers. "You spend too much time inside. Somedays, I wonder if you'd ever see the sun if I didn't open the blinds."

"I work indoors, and the sun doesn't appear that often in the Pacific Northwest, so I don't miss much."

"Today is gorgeous. Not a cloud in the sky."

"Beautiful. I hope tonight is clear."

"You've gotten into stargazing."

Jenny nodded. "Something Dare started."

Knowing he might be—or had been—looking at the same sky that night made her feel closer to him. Silly, but she went outside every night.

"You're still emailing?" Missy asked.

"Not as much as we texted. He's away for work, but we've kept in touch. It's nice to have a new friend."

Missy's gaze narrowed. "Are you sure that's all it is?"

"Yes, but..."

"What?"

Jenny thought about the way tingles filled her stomach whenever Dare's emails arrived. His words made her feel as if she were special to him. "Sometimes... it feels like we're more than friends."

"Are you okay with that?"

"More than I thought I'd be considering I know nothing about him. Maybe that's the appeal."

"Whether you two are friends or something else, he makes you happy, and that's all that matters to me."

"Thanks." Dare did make her happy.

Missy raised her chin and let the sun kiss her face. "This is the life. Hands in the dirt. Kittens asleep in the house. You next to me with a big smile on your face. It doesn't get much better than this."

Missy hadn't sounded this content in years, not

since before Rob's death. Jenny's heart overflowed with joy. Maybe her sister-in-law was finally finding some peace with what had happened. That was what Rob would have wanted.

Jenny wanted that for Missy, too. "After we finish and get the kittens fed again, let's go out to eat and see a movie."

"I'd love that. We haven't done something like that in—"

"Way too long."

Missy laughed. "We're a pair."

"Partners in crime."

"Yes, but if Homeland Security comes knocking due to your internet searches, you're on your own."

It was Jenny's turn to laugh. She wouldn't be surprised if she was on a government watch list due to her internet searches on explosives, weapons, coup d'états, espionage, untraceable poisons, bomb defusing, and a hundred other things she'd looked up to research her thrillers.

They continued planting the rest of the flowers— red, pink, yellow, and purple. The bright colors shouted summertime and fun.

Jenny brushed the dirt from her hands. "This is exactly what the yard needed. And me, too."

Missy beamed as she picked up the garden tools.

Jenny's cell phone rang, so she pulled it from the pocket of her shorts. The name "Dare" was written on her screen.

Her heart slammed against her rib cage. Anticipation surged through her. He must be home. "It's him."

"Dare?" Missy asked.

Nodding, Jenny raised the phone to her ear. "Hello?"

"This is Susan O'Rourke, Darragh's mother. Is this Jenny?"

Her brain froze, but at the same time, her body grew warmer.

"Jenny?" the woman asked.

Not woman. Dare's mother. "Yes, I'm Jenny."

"Darragh was in an accident. He was a passenger in a helicopter that went down. He's been evacuated to the Brooke Army Medical Center in San Antonio."

Her chest hurt as if a hundred-pound bag of potting soil had been dropped on top of her. The racing of her heart was more like a lit fuse ready to detonate. Unable to speak, she froze.

Words flashed through her mind.

Dare. Army. Injured. Evacuated.

Just like Rob.

A lump burned in the back of Jenny's throat.

Chills racked her body.

Except her brother had never made the trip back for medical treatment and a goodbye. She'd flown with Missy to Dover Air Force Base to receive Rob's flag-draped coffin instead.

The past and present crashed into one another. Jenny rocked back onto her bottom. "Is he going to be okay?

"Darragh had surgery before he arrived. He's had more since and needs another."

"Another surgery..." Jenny realized his mother had never said that he would be okay. As she hugged her knees to her chest with her free arm, she kept the phone plastered against her ear. She didn't want to miss a word.

"He's been asking for you."

"Me?" Her voice cracked. She didn't know what to say. "We...I..."

They'd never exchanged last names or photos, but since he'd gone away on his trip—most likely a deployment based on this new information—she felt as if each email had brought them closer. Did he feel the same?

"Darragh wants to talk to you." Susan sounded tired. "I'll hold the phone for him, but let me warn you, he's weak and on pain medication. He won't sound like himself."

Jenny had never heard his voice so had no idea what he sounded like.

"Okay." The word came out as a whisper.

Missy had concern written all over her face and moved closer, but she didn't say anything.

Noises sounded in the background. Voices, but Jenny couldn't make out what was being said.

"Jenny." He sounded shaky.

"Hi, Dare." She gripped the phone with her right hand. "It's nice to hear your voice."

"Same."

An image of Rob appeared in her mind. She took a deep breath. "You're in the military."

Missy gasped.

"Army. Ranger," he said.

Another chill shivered through Jenny. Her hands felt cold. "I've heard rangers are tough."

Missy held Jenny's left hand.

"I..." Dare's voice wavered. "I miss you."

She sighed. The raw emotion in his voice tugged at her heart. Melted it. "I've missed you, but you're in the States now. Everything will be okay."

"Thinking about you kept me from giving up. Kept me alive."

Her breath caught in her throat. She forced

herself to breathe. "Oh, Dare..."

"I want to see you."

She wanted to see him. "I'll text a pic—"

"No. In real life. Come to me."

Her ears rang. Her body shook. She was almost afraid to ask. "When?"

"Now."

The mix of hope and anguish in that one word tore at her. "You want me to come there?"

"Please."

Other than book signings and the vacation to Enchanted Island last year, she stayed close to home for Missy's sake. Adventure was left for the books Jenny wrote or read. She wasn't the kind of woman to hop on an airplane to go to someone she'd never met. But how could she say no when he was hurting and asking for her?

"I..."

"If you want to see him...then you need to go," Missy whispered. "I'll be okay."

That was the push Jenny needed. She *wanted* to go to Dare. She needed to go to him.

"Okay." Her wish upon a star had been for him to come home, but not like this. "I'll be there as soon as I can."

****

The trip to San Antonio took Jenny all day thanks to a three-hour delay during a layover in Salt Lake City. She rode a shuttle bus to the rental car place and stood in line at the counter. Her phone rang. It was Missy.

"I was following your flight online and saw that the plane landed a few minutes ago." Missy's call must be on speakerphone because she sounded like she was talking in a cave full of meowing kittens. "How are you?"

"Fine." Jenny was. Well, as fine as a person could be meeting someone for the first time after they'd been injured doing who knew what for their country. "I'm waiting to pick up the rental car."

"I'm relieved you're fine, but I'm worried."

"Your research last night proved Dare is legit." Missy hadn't wanted Jenny to fly off without knowing more and had even asked another Gold Star family—families who'd lost a loved one during a war—for help. "A few days ago, a Blackhawk helicopter went down in Central America with United States Army Rangers aboard."

"But that's *all* you know."

"It's enough." And it was for now.

Jenny stepped forward in the line. Three people were ahead of her to get cars.

"It's just..." Missy paused. Silence filled the line. "Neither of us had the chance to be with Rob after he was injured. He was gone too soon. But you spent days at the hospital after your parents' car accident. You've lost your entire family. Stuff might come up when you're with Dare."

"It's been a couple of years since I've had any nightmares or panic attacks. I've visited people at the hospital and been fine."

"Yes, but you need to be prepared in case something happens *this* time."

"I will." The concern in Missy's voice touched Jenny's heart. She didn't know what she would do without her. "But just so you know, I haven't lost my entire family. I still have you."

"We might be sisters-in-law, but we're also sisters of the heart." Missy's voice was full of love.

"For sure, and I'm glad you brought this up, but..." Jenny tried to put into words what she was feeling. "This is going to sound bizarre and I can't explain it, but I feel like I'm supposed to be here with Dare."

"I could tell when I dropped you off at the airport this morning, but please, be careful. He's still someone you don't really know, and you're a long way from home." The kittens got louder. "I need to fill more bottles with formula. Call me later."

"Will do." Jenny imagined the bundles of fur running around the kitchen. "Have fun with the kitten brigade."

Soon, Jenny had her rental car. She ate fast food—a burger and fries with a chocolate milkshake—for dinner, and then drove to the hospital.

Coming to San Antonio felt like the right thing to do, but she couldn't stop thinking about what Missy had said.

That's all you know.

Jenny gripped the steering wheel. She liked how she and Dare wrote each other. No last names. No details of what they did. Not a lot about real life. Just fun, advice, and some heartfelt sharing. Had they gotten closer over the weeks—almost two months of being in contact? Yes. Without a doubt. But once she met Dare face to face...

Her worst-case-scenario writer brain went into overdrive.

What if the man she'd gotten to know through his emails and texts hadn't been real? What if he'd crafted a persona the way she created characters in her books? What if...?

At Fort Sam Houston's visitor center, Jenny

presented her ID to receive a pass before driving to the hospital. She'd received a text—most likely from his mom—with Dare's room number. As she walked along a brightly lit hallway, Jenny's stomach felt fluttery, more nerves than anxiety, but she'd forgotten that feeling of uncertainty that seemed to hang in the air in hospitals.

She checked the room number of the nearest door. Not quite there yet, so she kept walking.

People spoke in hushed voices. A phone rang. Nurses entered and left rooms.

Jenny reached Dare's door, but she didn't go inside. What-ifs wracked her brain. Not bad ones like before but good ones. What if Dare turned out to be exactly the man she thought he was? What if her feelings for him got stronger once she saw him? What if she fell for him?

Being friends had been enough for her. It wasn't until the past couple of weeks that her feelings for Dare had been growing...changing. It made her wonder what he would think about her.

Interacting online was different from real life. With a keyboard to communicate, she could use words to her advantage to be funny or entertaining. In person, she came across as introverted and shy. He might not want anything to do with a quiet, boring author.

The thought poked her heart.

Jenny pushed her shoulders back.

Didn't matter what he thought about her.

That wasn't why she was here.

Come to me.

When?

Now.

It was time to stop procrastinating. Jenny knocked on Dare's door.

CHAPTER SIX

A FEMALE VOICE said, "Come in."

Jenny pushed open the door and walked into the hospital room. Beeps and blips sounded. The bed closest to her was empty but not the other.

Dare.

A tall woman with short, mahogany-colored hair blocked the view of the occupied bed. She wore jeans, a short-sleeved green blouse, and slip-on canvas shoes. Dark circles were under her puffy eyes.

"You must be Jenny." The woman smiled. "I'm Susan. I wish we were meeting under better circumstances, but thank you for coming to see Darragh."

Susan made this visit seem totally normal. If only...

"How is he?" Jenny asked.

"In and out. He had another surgery today. With all the hardware they're putting inside him, he'll be setting off metal detectors for the rest of his life."

Dare was alive. That was all that mattered. Jenny swallowed.

She walked toward the bed where a man lay. Wires connected him to machines that made noises and lit up. An IV line went into the top of his right hand. One leg was elevated in a traction device. A cast covered part of his left forearm and hand. A white bandage concealed half his forehead. Cuts and bruises marred his face and arms. But he still looked like...

Ash.

Her heart lurched.

She did a double take. Blinked. Refocused.

Not Ash.

Dare.

A hand touched her shoulder. Susan.

"Are you okay, Jenny?"

Not trusting her voice, she nodded, even though her world had tilted off its axis and was spinning out of control.

Dare was in his mid-to-late twenties and more gorgeous than she'd imagined Ash. Even with the injuries Dare had sustained. The way his features fit together was perfect.

Her pulse took off faster than the speed of light.

This was who found her bottle? Her BFF? Her...*friend*?

Susan gave her shoulder a squeeze and then lowered her hand. "It's so hard to see Darragh like this. He's always been so active and athletic. Rarely caught colds. He played wide receiver for his junior college football team. He could have transferred to a four-year university, but after he got his associate's degree, all he wanted to do was enlist and become a ranger."

Like Rob—only his dream had been to be a marine.

"Honorable," Jenny said, thinking of both men.

"That's Darragh." Susan's gaze traveled from him to Jenny. "You know my son well."

It didn't sound like a question. For that, Jenny was grateful because she wouldn't have known how to answer.

"He'll be so happy you're here," Susan added.

Jenny hoped so. "He looks young."

"Darragh always had such a baby face growing up. Even in high school. Now his sisters call him a pretty boy. He hates that." Susan laughed. "Twenty-six, and his sisters can still get to him."

Twenty-six. Five years younger than Jenny. Not that she didn't have friends of all ages. "He mentioned having three sisters."

"Yes, Kate was here for the first two days. She left

yesterday because she had to work. Claire and Fiona just started classes at their respective colleges, so I told them not to come. They're furious at me for that. At least Claire is in New Hampshire and can check on the house while I'm here. I did what I thought best and what Darragh would have wanted."

Interesting. All four kids had Irish names. Jenny wondered if Dare had grown up in New Hampshire. She'd never been there. "He's protective of his sisters."

"He's worse than a mama bear. Heaven help the guy who breaks one of their hearts." Susan yawned. "Excuse me."

Dare's mom looked tired. Being on her own with her injured son had to be difficult. That gave Jenny an idea.

"Why don't you take a break from the hospital tonight?" Missy had guaranteed Jenny's hotel reservation so all she would have to do was call and say she'd be checking in tomorrow. "I'll stay here with Dare so you can sleep."

"Are you sure you don't mind being here alone?"

"Not at all, and I'm not alone." Jenny looked at the man asleep in the bed. "Dare is here."

"Having a night away would be nice." Susan sounded relieved. "I...I haven't left the hospital much. I didn't want to leave him."

"There's no reason for us both to stay tonight."

Susan nodded. "Be warned—that chair isn't all that comfortable."

"One night should be okay, but several has probably worn out your back, neck, arms, and legs."

"Yes. I'm feeling my age." Susan laughed. "This will work out well. I'm sure Darragh would rather wake up to your pretty face than his old mom's."

Jenny's cheeks heated. She wasn't so sure since he'd never seen her. "You're not old. And he looks like he won't be awake much tonight."

"In the morning, then."

She and Dare would be spending their first night together. Well, sort of. Wait until Missy heard. Jenny almost laughed. "Go eat non-hospital food and sleep."

"You don't have to tell me again." Susan picked up a large, lime-green tote bag. She reached inside and pulled out a business card. "Here's my cell number. I put yours into my contacts yesterday."

"Okay." Susan must be the organized type. The only reason Jenny's life flowed smoothly was because of Missy, who kept track of well, everything, so Jenny could focus on writing. "I'll call if there's anything you should know."

Susan kissed the right side of Dare's forehead where there wasn't a bandage or bruise. "I'll be back in the morning if I don't hear from you tonight."

Jenny smiled. "Goodnight."

"Try to get some sleep. And thanks for giving me a night off." With that, Susan walked out of the room. The door closed behind her.

Jenny blew out a breath. "It's just you and me, Dare."

He didn't stir.

She walked to his bed, removed her bag from her shoulder, and set it next to the chair. Maybe she could work on outlining her next book, *Assassin Curse*. She pulled out her spiral notebook and pen but then put them back into her tote. There would be time to work later. All she wanted to do was stare at Dare.

His arms lay outside the blanket. Part of a tattoo showed at the bottom of his sleeve. He was tall and fit, but he looked so vulnerable lying in the hospital bed.

"I'd give anything to make you all better."

Jenny touched his thumb on the hand with the IV in it. That seemed a safer choice than the arm with the cast.

His skin was warm. Calloused and scarred, too.

He stirred.

She jerked her hand away. "Dare?"

His eyes remained closed. "Jenn..."

Her heart raced. "I'm here. I'm right here, Dare."

She couldn't imagine being anywhere else. That should send off warning bells and flashing caution lights, but she didn't mind.

As Jenny pushed the chair closer to the bed, she kept her gaze on Dare. They had never met, but she felt as if she knew him. His emails and texts had filled something that was missing inside her. That was why she'd kept writing back and getting excited when she heard from him.

Friendship, yes, that had been part of it, but there was more. Jenny liked the Dare she'd gotten to know from his correspondence, and she cared what happened to him. She couldn't deny her physical attraction, either. Something that made her feel weird given he was injured and in the hospital. She shouldn't be thinking he was hot.

Sitting, she leaned closer to the bed and released a long sigh.

"It looks like my message in the bottle did bring me my dream hero."

Jenny didn't know whether to laugh or cry...because she had a sinking feeling she'd have a better shot at dating Bigfoot than Dare O'Rourke.

CHAPTER SEVEN

WHAT WAS GOING on? Dare opened his eyes. The light hit like a sledgehammer, so he squeezed his eyelids shut.

Noises sounded. Mechanical ones. Beeping.

Some sounded at a set interval. Others randomly.

His body felt...different. Weird. Unattached. Floating like a balloon let loose in the sky. Well, a balloon that had survived a hurricane *and* a meteor shower.

His head throbbed. A dull ache filled his stomach. A pressure built in his arms and legs. Or was that his hip? He couldn't tell.

The pain felt as if it were distant, no longer in his face—raw, intense, jagged—as it once had been. He remembered that much. He tried to remember more.

The beeping increased.

Weird. His mind seemed to be a patchwork of memories. Pieces sewn loosely together.

Someone pressed against Dare's leg. Movement.

Machinery cutting into metal. Yelling. Hearing the 9 Line MEDEVAC Request over the chaos.

For some reason, line three had stuck with Dare: "One Alpha, three Bravo, four Charlie, one Delta."

Urgent, urgent surgical, priority, routine.

Dare had no idea which of the nine patients he'd been. He hoped he'd been the alpha. If he'd been the most seriously injured, then the others would be doing better than him and recovering quickly.

Recovering where?

He blinked open his eyes to find out. The light was still bright, but it wasn't as blaring as the first time he'd tried.

He was in a hospital, but he'd already guessed that. Which hospital, or even which country, he wasn't sure. Panama? America?

Machines with wires and cables attached to him made the noises. He listened closer. Someone was in the room. He could hear breathing.

As he turned his head toward the sound, a knife dug into his brain. Okay, not really, but moving his head hurt worse than a whiskey hangover.

A woman was asleep in a chair. She sat sideways with her knees over the chair arm. Her head was angled downward. Long, caramel-colored hair with blond highlights covered her face.

Dare could make out pale, smooth skin and full lips, but that was it. He didn't recognize her coloring or hair, but he liked what he saw.

Who was she? And why was she here?

A door opened. Footsteps sounded on the tile floor.

He tried to use his peripheral vision to see who'd entered, but couldn't. "Hello?"

His voice sounded rough. No kidding, his mouth felt as if it were stuffed with cotton.

"You're awake," a familiar voice said.

That sounded like his... "Mom? What are you doing here?"

"Where else would I be?"

And then he remembered. His mom had been here for a few days. He'd forgotten that and what else she'd said had happened.

A Blackhawk had picked up him and his squad. They were en route to get Hamilton and the others when the helicopter went down.

Dare's jaw clenched. "Any word on my guys?"

"Yang was released yesterday. He stopped by before he left and wants to talk when you feel up to it. Humphreys is improving every day. I spoke to his mom at the support center while you were in surgery. Garcia is still critical."

"The flight crew?"

"I don't know, honey. I asked, but getting answers isn't easy."

No news had to be good news. If anyone had died, it would be in the papers. Still, he wanted to find out about the crew.

His mom stood at the side of the bed. "Looks like Jenny got some sleep."

Jenny.

The air rushed from Dare's lungs. He couldn't breathe. A machine beeped faster.

His mom touched his arm. "Relax, honey. You had a collapsed lung."

He tried to calm himself. Focused on his breathing as if he were taking aim for a shot. Air went in and out. The beeping slowed.

Dare stared at the woman—Jenny—sleeping in the chair. "Why is she here?"

"You asked her to come."

"I did?" His mind was a blank.

"You kept calling for her. Over and over. You woke up long enough to tell me the passcode on your phone so that I could call her. You spoke with her for a minute."

"I don't remember."

"That's okay. You're hurting. Having surgeries. On

pain meds."

Maybe that memory would come back to him like some of the others, but only one thing mattered now. Jenny was *here*.

He stared at her. "What do you think about Jenny?"

"I can see why you're so taken with her. As soon as she arrived, she said she'd stay here and sent me on my way. I didn't realize how much I needed a full night's sleep in a bed. Not that I haven't wanted to be here with you."

"I understand, Mom."

His mom glanced at Jenny before looking back at him. "You haven't mentioned her. Is this something new?"

"Since early July. I..." His face warmed. He wasn't sure what to say that wouldn't sound crazy to his mom. "We live in different states."

"She must care to have dropped everything and flown here to be with you."

"Yeah."

"She's older than I thought she'd be."

Dare didn't care. "Age is just a number."

"Oh, sweetie, I didn't mean anything by that, but you're right. A few years doesn't make a difference. As long as she's not like Kayla."

"She's nothing like her." The words came out harsher than he'd intended, but Jenny didn't deserve to be compared to his ex-girlfriend in any way.

Dare might not remember asking Jenny to come, but he knew why he would have. She'd been on his mind constantly. Maybe she'd felt the shift in their emails like he had. Not quite intimate, but they'd shared more private things, and a closeness had developed over these past weeks. One that hadn't been there before he'd deployed.

His mother held a large plastic cup with a lid and a straw up to his mouth, and he sipped. "You haven't stopped looking at her."

A Humvee seemed to be parked on his chest. "I missed her."

He missed texting her. When they were replying in real time, it almost felt as if they were talking to each other. They hadn't seemed like they were on opposite sides of the country. He'd liked that.

His mother set the cup on the bed table. "Based on the way Jenny was staring at you last night, I'd say the feeling is mutual."

Dare felt warm all over.

Jenny stirred. Stretched. Opened her eyes. Straightened.

She pushed the hair off her face.

The force of seeing her hit Dare hard. The blips and beeps from the machines accelerated.

Oh, man, she was beautiful. High cheekbones and lips made for slow, hot kisses.

Her tangled hair and not-quite-awake eyes made her look sleep-rumpled adorable. He fought the urge to reach out to her. To touch her to make sure she wasn't a fantasy. If she wasn't real, she was part of the best dream ever.

Her green-eyed gaze met his. "Good morning."

Emotion tightened his throat. He tried to lift his head, but it hurt too much. "Come closer."

Jenny stood and stepped forward until she was right at the edge of his bed.

Dare reached up with his good arm. The one with bruises, cuts, and an IV. He touched her shoulder to prove to himself she wasn't an illusion.

A burst of heat rushed up the length of his arm at the point of contact. Not a dream—*real*. "You're here."

"You asked me to come."

"I don't remember." He felt like an idiot. "I'm sorry."

Her gaze hadn't wavered, and Dare was glad about that. He could stare into her green eyes for days.

Jenny.

The emotions running through him had nothing

to do with friendship. Not even close. They weren't brand new feelings, if he was being honest with himself. They just seemed clearer now that the two of them were together.

"That's okay," she said, and he had no doubt she meant it.

It *was* okay. With Jenny next to him, everything felt better. "I never found out the real name of your star."

"We can do that together when you feel better."

"Thank you for staying here last night," his mom said. "I haven't slept so well in days."

"Anytime," Jenny said.

"I'm going to grab a cup of coffee from the cafeteria. I forgot to get one on my way up." His mom's smile brightened her face. "Would you like a cup, Jenny?"

Jenny nodded. "I'd love one with cream and sugar, please."

"I'll be back." His mom walked out the door.

Holding up his arm was getting harder to do. He hated showing any sign of weakness because he needed to be strong. People counted on him—his mom, his sisters, his guys, and now Jenny. He ran his fingertips along her smooth skin until he reached her hand. He could rest his arm on the bed this way.

"Thank you for coming." Though he hated her seeing him in pain, on meds, and not in control of...anything. "This must be weird for you."

"A little, but I figured it might be."

He appreciated her honesty. "Is Missy okay with you being away?"

"Yes, we talked after I arrived. She knows I want to be here, and she told me she'd be okay. I'm confident she will be. She seems more content than she's been since my brother passed."

That was good news. Dare could tell Jenny was pleased, and it made him happy.

He rubbed his thumb against her hand. "I can't believe you came all this way, and I don't even know your last name."

"Hanford."

Jenny Hanford. "Mine's O'Rourke."

"Your mom told me."

"Oh, right."

"How do you feel?" Jenny asked.

The concern in her voice and eyes wrapped around him like a hug. "Better now that you're here."

A smile spread across her face, reaching all the way to her eyes. The result was breathtaking.

"You're beautiful, Jenny. I mean, I thought you were before I saw you, but you are in person, too."

Circles of red formed on her cheeks.

"I'm sorry." Dare had embarrassed her and himself. "We're friends, but I'm getting all gushy."

"I like gushy."

That was a relief. "But I'm not making sense."

"For someone who's been injured, you're doing great." She bent over. "Now that you're awake, I want to give you something."

His gaze went straight to her jean-clad butt. Oh, yeah. He nearly laughed. Guess he wasn't *that* hurt if he was noticing how sexy she was.

Jenny held a bag. "It's from Berry Lake. That's where I live. Home of the Huckleberry Festival and the Bigfoot Seeker Gathering."

Berry Lake, Washington. He hoped he remembered the name of her hometown.

She tilted the bag toward him. He reached in with his right hand since his left was useless. His fingers pushed through tissue paper until he touched something soft and...furry.

What...

Dare pulled out a stuffed animal. Not any animal. A ten-inch Bigfoot. He laughed, even though it hurt his stomach and his head.

Her green eyes twinkled. "I couldn't resist."

"I'm glad you didn't." He placed the Sasquatch

next to him in bed and then touched her hand again. "My very own Squatchy. Thanks."

His eyelids felt heavy. He struggled to keep them open.

Jenny pulled his blanket up. "You're getting tired."

"I want to keep talking to you, but I'm losing the battle."

"Sleep."

Dare didn't want to let go of her hand. He was used to taking care of everyone in his family and squad, but today, for the first time in a long time, he could ask for what he wanted and not feel guilty. "Stay."

"I'm not going anywhere." As if to reaffirm her words, Jenny laced her fingers between his. "I promise."

Not that he hadn't believed her before, but when Dare closed his eyes, he knew she would be there when he woke. It was the best feeling ever.

CHAPTER EIGHT

THE DAYS BLURRED into each other. Dare's condition continued to improve. Jenny wrote while he slept or had appointments with various therapists, but she was relieved to be at the start of a new story and not on deadline. Daily calls with Missy reminded Jenny there was life outside of the hospital and kept her on track with to-do items she could check off the list. Brief visits to the hotel gave hints at the sights San Antonio had to offer, but Jenny didn't want to play tourist. She preferred being with Dare. He seemed to feel the same way.

He liked falling asleep with his hand on hers. Whenever he woke, the first thing he did was look for her. Knowing how much he wanted her to be with him gave her a rush.

Not that they'd done anything other than hold hands, but she was learning more about him each day. His favorite color was blue—the same color of his gorgeous eyes. He loved watching football. He ate hot dogs with mustard and relish. Christmas was his favorite holiday.

When she returned to the hospital after a quick trip to her hotel, Jenny couldn't wait to find out how Dare had done at physical therapy. She walked into the room and found him sipping water from a straw. Squatchy sat against the pillow.

"Where's your mom?" Jenny asked.

"Coffee break. She's addicted."

Susan did like her coffee.

Dare was smiling. His bruises had faded to a yellow color. Some of the scratches had healed. The stubble on his face gave him a sexy, bad-boy edge. "Guess what?"

"You saw a UFO," she joked.

"Better."

"Better than a UFO?" She set her purse next to the chair. "I'm all ears."

"I got to talk to one of my guys. Ethan Humphreys. Nice kid from Peoria, Illinois. He's recovering and should be heading home soon."

The relief and happiness in Dare's voice made Jenny feel warm all over. She reached out and touched his hand. "I'm so glad to hear that."

Dare nodded. "Lee Yang is already home, so that just leaves Carlos Garcia. I haven't been able to talk to him. Humphreys told me Carlos was messed up bad."

She gave Dare a squeeze. Between his leg, hip, and arm injuries, he couldn't get around in narrow or small spaces. "You'll see Carlos once you're up and about."

"I'm going to keep asking until they get tired of saying no and let me in."

"I'm sure you could sweet talk a nurse."

He raised a brow. "You think?"

"Definitely."

"I'm not much of a charmer, but I might have to give that a try for Carlos' sake."

Dare oozed charm, but she loved that he didn't realize it. "How did PT go?"

He set the cup on the bed tray. "I'm still limited with what I can do, but those surgeons managed to save my leg. I'm going to show my gratitude by working my butt off to recover ASAP."

He sounded determined. She gazed at his arms, the only parts other than his neck and head not covered. "You look fit to me."

That brow shot up again. "Like what you see?"

Dare's flirtatious tone matched the gleam in his eyes. Sometimes, he seemed so young and innocent with the way he kept Squatchy nearby and wanted her close to him, a one-eighty from a man who was a member of a special operations elite infantry unit and in charge of a squad. But then, something would change. A smoldering look would flash across his face that was all male and heated her from the inside.

"Fishing for compliments?" she asked.

"Always from pretty girls."

She laughed. "I'll take pretty, but I'm thirty-one. Long past the girl stage."

"You're not past anything," Dare countered. "My granny calls my mom 'girl.' And thirty-one is only a couple of years older than me."

"Five."

"That's a couple."

"More like a few."

"Few is good." He reached for the TV remote sitting next to the cup on the bed tray. "Let's see what's on TV."

"Remember what the doctor said? No electronics for a few more days due to your head injury. That includes watching TV."

"I'm not watching." He used the remote to change the channel. "You are."

"What will you do?"

"Watch you."

"Very funny." Except...he *was* looking at her.

"Look what's on."

The opening credits for *Finding Bigfoot* filled the

television hanging on the far wall.

"No way." She laughed. "This is one of my favorite shows. How did you know it was on?"

"I had a feeling you might watch this series. I asked a nurse to find out what time it aired."

Jenny's heart bumped. Dare was injured and hurting, as was his team, yet he was thinking about her. So sweet. "Thanks. Keep this up, and I'll be crushing on you big time."

"You aren't already?" He feigned being sad with an exaggerated frown.

"Well, maybe a little."

"I'm going to have to turn the *little* into *a lot*."

Electricity crackled between them. Tension built.

If Jenny wasn't careful, having a crush on Dare would be the least of her worries. She angled the chair so it was closer to the bed and gave her a better view of the television.

"You can't see the TV as well from the chair." Dare patted the space to the right of him. "There's enough room here."

No, there wasn't. She stiffened. Space, that was. They'd be crammed, an entire side of their bodies touching.

Anticipation surged. Okay, the thought held a *certain* appeal.

Stop. Bad idea. "I don't want to hurt you."

"You won't." He sounded confident. "You'll be more comfortable, and so will I. You can keep me warm."

She gave him a look. "I can get you another blanket if you're cold."

"I don't want a blanket." His eyes darkened. "I want you."

Jenny's pulse sprinted. Her mouth went dry. She adjusted the bottom of her T-shirt to give her time to control her excitement.

She held in a grin. "Is this how you watch TV with your friends?"

"No, but we flew past the just-friends stage a few weeks into my deployment." He patted the mattress again. "Get up here."

Dare went after what he wanted. Which, right now, seemed to be her. She was okay with that.

Jenny climbed onto the bed, careful where she placed her hands and legs. She was trying to protect Dare's injuries and herself. The width of the bed didn't allow her to lie flat on her back, so she was on her left side. She kept a few inches between them, so their bodies weren't plastered against each other.

"Isn't this better?" he asked, sounding satisfied.

Better wasn't the word she would use. Her heart

beat triple time. Every nerve ending tingled. She doubted her pulse would slow by tomorrow morning.

"Are you sure this is okay with your injuries?" she asked.

"Yes, except for one thing."

Oh, no. Her muscles bunched. She must be hurting him somehow. "What?"

He put his arm around her and pulled her closer. The space between them disappeared. "This will keep the IV line from being smooshed by accident."

Smooth move, Sergeant O'Rourke.

Jenny could imagine Ash doing something similar. Her front pressed against his right side. He might be injured, but he was solid.

Heat emanated from him. No way had he been cold.

Of course not. She had underestimated Dare, but this side of him was sexy. "You have this all figured out."

"I'm highly trained. Skilled in rapid responses and direct action."

"I can only imagine your...talents."

Mischief flashed in his eyes. "I'll show you..."

Temptation flared, but Jenny wasn't ready for that. Not yet. She stared at the television. "The commercials are over."

"Bigfoot really is my competition." Dare's tone was playful. As he looked at her and not the TV, he rubbed her arm as if it was the most normal thing in the world to do.

The way his fingertips caressed her skin distracted her, but she couldn't deny his touch felt oh-so-good. Had seduction techniques been part of his training?

"Have you seen this episode?" he asked.

Ignoring the tingles his touch brought, she focused on the screen. "No, but I'm behind. I'm a binge watcher."

"Me, too. That way, I don't get caught up on cliffhangers. Not a fan of those."

Watching a show could wait. Jenny wanted to learn more about Dare. She picked up the remote and turned off the television.

"I thought you wanted to watch this," he said.

"I'd rather talk to you."

That charming grin of his returned with a vengeance, and her breath caught in her throat. "I'm all yours."

If only... She almost laughed. "What TV shows do you watch when you are home?"

"Whatever's on Netflix. No TV. I moved into the barracks about a year and a half ago. It was only supposed to be temporary, but I'm still there."

"What's it like to live in the barracks?"

"Like being the oldest guy in a dorm." He laughed. "Not really. I've never lived in a dorm. But I had no other choice. My former roommate was my best friend, and I was renting a room from him."

Her lips parted. She remembered what Dare had texted about his best friend. "You lost your best friend, your girlfriend, and the place you lived?"

Dare nodded. "I didn't put up much of a fight. I just wanted...out."

Jenny had a feeling there was more to the story. "How do you feel now?"

"Like I dodged a bullet." No regret sounded in his voice or showed on his face. "I'm happy how things have turned out and where I am. Especially now that I'm here with you."

His words made her happy because she felt the same way. Hard to believe she hadn't known Dare existed at the beginning of July, and now she was rarely away from him.

"What about you?" he asked. "Any ghosts in your relationship closet?"

He'd been open with her. It was her turn. "I was engaged three years ago. I found out a couple of weeks before the wedding that he had a gambling problem and owed a lot of money. Almost two hundred thousand."

"Whoa."

"That was my thought." She shook her head. "He felt I should help pay off his debt. I disagreed. Things went downhill from there, and we broke up."

"That had to be hard so close to your wedding."

"Yes, but he was with me for all the wrong reasons. I just hadn't realized it. I still feel foolish for being taken in like that, but I know I dodged a bullet."

"Everything happens for a reason."

She thought of her brother dying for his country and her parents who'd died after a head-on collision. "You think so? Because that hasn't been my experience."

"I'll add the word sometimes," Dare said. "Look at us. I wish my squad and I had never gotten injured, but if I was still with the platoon, I wouldn't be here with you, and I wouldn't have Squatchy as my new sidekick. Maybe there was a reason this time."

"I'd like to think so in our case."

"She agrees with me, Squatchy," Dare said to the stuffed animal. "That's a good sign."

His smile crinkled his eyes, and the result took her breath away. He was so hot. The best-looking man she'd ever met. Dare could be with any woman. Why her?

Just enjoy being with him while it lasts.

"Speaking of Sasquatch," he continued. "Did you know there have been Bigfoot sightings around Joint Base Lewis-McChord that's south of Tacoma? Stories have also circulated about Cat Lake and other places used for training," Dare said. "Though it could just be an urban legend."

"I hadn't heard that about JBLM, but the Pacific Northwest is full of sightings. Our town has capitalized on the ones around Berry Lake. There's a shop that offers Bigfoot tours and searches to tourists."

"You're kidding?"

"Nope. Bigfoot is big business in Berry Lake."

"When I visit, we can go on one of those searches."

Not if or maybe, but when. Anticipation surged. Jenny would love to show Dare around her hometown. "That would be fun."

"I can think of something else that would be fun."

Her gaze met his, but his face gave nothing away.

"A game of cards?" she asked.

"Nope."

"Twenty questions?"

"Try again."

Until he improved a little more, they were limited on where they could go or what they could do. "A walk?"

"I'm quite comfy where I am." Of course he was. And if he kept scooting her closer, she would end up on top of him. Although, that might be his plan.

"I have no idea," she said. "What?"

"This." Dare captured her lips with his. She inhaled sharply, caught off guard. Did this count as direct action or perhaps a rapid response?

Whatever it was, Dare could kiss.

His lips tested and tasted and teased.

Highly skilled, yes.

The way his mouth moved over hers made Jenny want more. She arched closer.

Her fingers itched to touch him, but she wasn't sure what was safe and what would hurt him, so she kept her hands to herself.

Not that she needed more than his lips against hers.

He tasted sweet and warm with a hint of peppermint.

As he pressed harder, she parted her lips.

No one had ever kissed her like Dare. She felt desired and cherished. In his kiss, she found a sense of belonging...as if she'd come home.

He pulled back, not far, just enough so he could gaze into her eyes. The hunger in his matched what she felt coursing through her body.

"I've been wanting to do that." His voice was as tender as a caress.

Her lips tingled. "Me, too."

"We're going to have to keep doing that."

He'd get no disagreement from her. "Sounds like a plan."

And he kissed her again.

CHAPTER NINE

A FEW DAYS later, the sun beat down on Dare's face. The temperature felt more like August than September, but he had no complaints. He tilted his head back to smile at Jenny as she pushed his wheelchair toward a bench at the edge of a grassy area.

He inhaled, taking in the scents of the outdoors. Just what he needed. "It's a gorgeous afternoon. Thanks for getting me outside."

"The fresh air is good for you."

She was good for him.

Grateful didn't begin to describe how he felt for finding that bottle on the beach or to Staff Sergeant Hamilton for telling Dare to reply or to his mom for calling Jenny. Dare had never believed in fate before, but something extra seemed to be in play here.

"You deserve a change in scenery," she added. "What you're going through can't be easy."

It wasn't. "Having you here helps."

"And your guys."

"It's only Carlos and me now."

Humphreys had been shipped to Columbus yesterday, even though he'd asked to stay with Dare and Garcia. An order was an order, but Dare understood why Ethan felt that way and reminded him that Yang was back at Fort Benning and might want to see him.

Jenny set the brakes on the wheelchair before coming around to sit on the bench. "You've been doing a great job to make the best of your situation, which has helped your mom. But I know you've been worried about your squad, especially Carlos. Please don't feel the need to pretend in front of me."

"Why would you think I'm pretending?"

"Because even though you seem like a superhero, you're very much human."

That was something he'd been reminded of every single day since the crash. He'd been in firefights and raids. Yeah, he'd been shot at and grazed by bullets. But he'd never really thought about dying until now.

"There's no reason to tell everyone how I feel."

Especially her. She might not like seeing him that way. He didn't want her thinking he was less of a man.

Dare blew out a breath.

"You can't hold it all in," she said. "At some point, it'll come out. Please, talk to me."

He wanted to say no. That nothing was wrong. But he'd be lying to her if he did that. His father had done nothing but lie and withhold information before he'd deserted the family. Dare tried hard not to have anything in common with him except his gender and last name.

"I haven't been pretending. I just haven't shared everything I'm thinking," Dare admitted. "They brought in a head doctor for me to talk with after I got upset during one of my therapy sessions."

Jenny held his hand. "I'm glad you've had someone to talk to, but I'm here also. Don't forget that."

"I can't forget you."

"Except for asking me to come see you." She brushed her lips across his. "Joking."

In the distance, laughter sounded.

Dare looked across the grass. A pretty, pregnant brunette held the hand of a toddler. The little girl skipped and bounced on the sidewalk. Next to them was a man with no legs in an electric wheelchair. He was smiling and saying something to the little girl, who was giggling.

Dare shook his head. "I don't mean to shut you out. It's just others have it worse than me."

"Maybe you weren't injured as badly as others

have been, but you're still affected by this. Physically and emotionally. You can't downplay how you feel because you don't want to worry people or believe you have to act strong all the time."

He stared at the grass. "My mom's been through so much. My dad's no longer in the picture. Hasn't been since I was thirteen. But even before then, he wasn't around much. She's done so much for my sisters and me, and now she's put her life on hold to be here. You have, too."

"We're here because we care about you, Dare. There's no place I'd rather be, and your mom feels the same way. We want to help you, but you have to let us do that."

"I know." If there was anyone Dare could talk to, it was Jenny. "But my dad used to complain. About everything."

"You wouldn't be complaining. You're just letting what's inside out."

"You make it sound easy."

She shrugged. "You won't know if it is or not until you try."

Dare had a feeling she could talk him into anything. He took a breath. And another.

"I hate this. Being injured. Stuck in a hospital. Unable to help my guys. Relying on everyone but myself." He half-laughed. "Those sound like complaints."

"You're being honest. Keep going."

Saying the words aloud released some of the tension in his shoulders. He wanted to keep going. "I keep thinking about my staff sergeant. His name is Hamilton. He's still deployed with the others. I miss Mitch and the rest of the guys so freaking much. I can't wait to hear they're home." Dare shifted. "The crash wasn't my fault, but I feel like I've let my guys down. That I should have been able to keep them safe. I want a do-over, so I can change what's happened. But I can't, and it feels like there's this ball or something stuck at the back of my throat. It just keeps hurting."

She stood, walked to the back of his wheelchair, and put her arms around him. "I wish there were do-overs, too."

Dare sank into Jenny's embrace. He just wanted to be held. Her warm breath against his neck was added comfort.

"Wanting to be with my platoon doesn't mean I don't want to be with you, too. You have a way of making me feel better without even trying. It's confusing to want to be here and there at the same time."

She raised his hand and kissed it. "I'm sure it is

confusing and frustrating, but all you need to focus on right now is healing. Your recovery is the most important thing."

He knew Jenny was correct, but that didn't make his feelings any easier to deal with. "The head doctor said something similar."

She squeezed his hand. "Talk to the doctor. Talk to your mom. Talk to me. Call your guys or your staff sergeant."

Dare nodded.

Jenny kept hold of him. "We haven't known each other long—"

"It feels like I've known you forever."

"Same." He couldn't see her face, but he knew she was smiling. "We joke around a lot, and I have no idea what you're going through, but please know you can talk to me about anything. I might not have the answers, but I can listen. It takes a strong man to tell someone what he's feeling. That's not a weakness."

Dare's gut told him Jenny would be there no matter if things were going well or if he were struggling. That he could trust her no matter what. She wouldn't hurt him the way others had. "The same goes for you."

He thought she'd let go of him and return to the bench, but she didn't. Having her hold him felt so good. Words didn't seem necessary. Just being together was enough.

A bee flew across the tops of the blades of grass. A siren sounded in the distance. Peals of laughter filled the air as the little girl twirled across the grass with her arms extended until the woman called for her.

"That little girl is so cute," Jenny said. "Not a care in the world."

Dare wondered what Jenny's kids might look like. Mini versions of her if they were lucky. A question popped into his head. "Do you want kids?"

"Yes, but..."

He looked at her. She had a puzzled expression on her face. "What?"

"I wrote about having a family in my last email to you. The one about Missy's foster kittens."

Dare had read her emails so many times he had them memorized. "I never saw that one. What did it say?"

"You really want to know?"

"You bet."

Removing her cell from her pocket, she returned to the bench and sat. "The email is in my sent folder."

"Read it to me, please."

"Dear BFF."

As Dare listened to her email, he had no doubt if

he hadn't already fallen for Jenny, he would be now. Who was he kidding? He was tumbling head-first.

Wishing on a star. Eating a special brownie for the two of them. Falling in love with kittens. Having an old-fashioned life plan—one that sounded perfect to him.

Where had this woman been all his life? And how did he get her to move to Fort Benning so they could be together?

Dare's injuries were improving, and he would be able to return to duty in time. He hadn't decided if he would be career military or not yet, but he knew one thing. He wanted her with him wherever that might be. There was no way he was letting Jenny go. But first things first...

"Did you make a decision about adopting a kitten?" he asked.

"No, I ended up coming here, and I honestly haven't thought about it again."

"Still want my advice?"

"Please."

"A pet won't mess up your plan, not as long as you stick to your list. Don't date men with allergies. Cats are independent. They are easier to leave than dogs if you want to go somewhere."

"I don't travel that much."

"And I quote 'Prefer armchair traveling to jet-setting.' Yet, you're here in San Antonio. If I'm going to visit Berry Lake, I hope you'd want to come to Columbus, Georgia."

Her eyes widened, but in a good way. That pleased him.

"I would like to visit you there," she said.

"Many cats are small enough to fit in a carrier under the seat in an airplane, too. You could bring the cat with you if you wanted."

He'd gone from being single, to having a girlfriend, to having a girlfriend with a cat. Funny, but he was fine with that. He'd need a pet friendly apartment or maybe a house.

"You think I should get a kitten?" she asked.

"I think you want one, and if so, I say go for it." Her smile told him he'd given the right advice, but he had one more thing to add. "And in case you're wondering, I'm not allergic to any animals."

CHAPTER TEN

THE NEXT MORNING, Dare raised his glass of orange juice. "Here's to improving enough to get a new room."

"Hear, hear." His mom drank. "Do you think you'll have a roommate?"

"No idea, but most likely."

He hadn't shared a bedroom in years, but how bad could it be? The nurses were always in and out to check on him. And anyone would be better considering what his last roommate did to him.

"Feel free to head out," he said. "I'm going to visit Garcia, and then I'll wait here for Jenny to show up later."

"Your sisters want to meet her."

"They will once I'm better."

"You sound certain."

"I am." He remembered what Jenny had said about letting his feelings out. "I've never felt like this about anyone. Not even close with Kayla. Yesterday, Jenny told me I shouldn't keep everything inside and pretend I'm okay."

"Smart woman. Your father was the master at keeping secrets. I had to drag everything out of him."

"Then I'm glad I opened up. I'm going to do everything I can so I don't screw up."

This time, his mom raised her juice. "To not screwing up."

Dare laughed. "Geez, Mom. Got any better advice than that?"

"Be open and honest. Trust and commitment go a long way to making a relationship work." His mom sipped the juice. "Your dad wasn't good at those things. I could only do so much."

His parents' arguments had ranged from money to where his father had gone after work instead of coming home. They'd never fought in front of Dare or his sisters, but their voices carried through the small house where he'd grown up. The same house where his mom still lived now. "I remember the fighting."

"I'm sorry you do." Regret filled her voice. "Your father was a damaged man. It wasn't all his fault, but he couldn't learn to move beyond any slight or hurt. His leaving was the best thing for us. I'll always be grateful to him for giving you and your sisters to me, though."

There was no remorse in her voice, just sincerity, even if his father leaving had meant his mom working three jobs for the first couple of years.

"You're the best. I love you, Mom," Dare said. He probably didn't say that enough, either.

A nurse entered the room. "Good morning. Corporal Garcia asked to see you. Want to pay him a visit?"

"Yes. I'm ready." If his mom hadn't been here, Dare would have answered with a four-letter word followed by a *yeah*. Mom hated when he swore.

"Tell Carlos I said hi." His mom kissed his cheek. "I'll be back later."

After donning yellow disposable scrubs, a mask, and gloves, Dare was wheeled into Garcia's room.

Carlos' eyes were closed, and his lips drawn into a thin line. He looked nothing like the cocky kid who thought he knew everything.

The nurse pushed Dare closer, locked the brake, and then left.

Dare was happy to be alone with the corporal. "You're getting the VIP treatment, Garcia. They made me get all dressed up to see you."

Carlos' eyes sprang open. Widened. A huge smile spread across his face. "Sergeant, you're okay."

The relief and happiness in Garcia's voice made Dare's throat burn and his eyes sting. "Getting there. Can't let you have all the attention."

"Someone has to get the hot nurses."

That sounded more like the ranger Dare knew. "That would be you."

"But don't tell Elle." Carlos lowered his voice as if someone might hear him. "She gets jealous."

Elle was Carlos' pretty fiancée. "Is she here?"

"She was. My mom's here now. They're going to take turns. I may have an extended stay ahead of me."

"Doesn't matter." Dare knew there was spinal cord damage. "You've got this."

"Going to give it my best shot, Sergeant." Carlos sounded optimistic. That was a good sign. "Is your mom here?"

He nodded. "She says hi."

"Did she bring cookies?"

Dare had forgotten that Carlos loved cookies. "No, but I'll ask if she can make some for you. She mentioned something about kitchen facilities at the family support center."

"Sweet. Is Jenny here, too?"

Hearing one of his guys mention her name so easily felt weird yet right. "Yes, she is."

"Just friends. Yeah, right." Carlos laughed and then grimaced. Pain? "I knew there was more going on. Yang owes me fifty bucks."

Dare's mouth gaped. "You bet on my friendship

with Jenny?"

"Relationship, and well, yeah."

He shook his head. "I'm going to come up with some kind of payback for when you get out of here."

"Bring it on, Sergeant. I'll be ready." Carlos' eyes gleamed. "It's good to see you."

Dare touched his arm. "I would have been here sooner, but I wouldn't fit with the traction junk they had me wearing. Now, I'll be here as often as you want company."

Carlos blinked. "That might be a lot, Sergeant."

"Then it's a lot."

He gripped the bedding. "I don't remember what happened. Do you?"

"Very little, but maybe Yang and Humphreys do and can fill in some blanks."

"It doesn't matter, but I'd still like to know, Sergeant."

"I know." Dare also knew Carlos needed him. Not a problem. That was why Dare was there. He stretched out his good leg to make himself comfortable. "Have you been watching any baseball games?"

****

Jenny hadn't set her alarm, so she shouldn't have

been surprised she'd slept until ten. Guess she needed the sleep after working on her new story last night. The words had been flowing. Ash had landed a sabotaged 777, and she hadn't wanted to stop.

With her arms over her head, she stretched.

No more being lazy. Time to get up so she could go back to the hospital. The more time she spent with Dare, the more she wanted to be with him.

Jenny touched her lips. She enjoyed his kisses, too.

Talking about his feelings yesterday hadn't been easy for him. She hadn't meant to push, but he couldn't keep everything inside and keep pretending he was fine. Missy had tried to do that and was still processing through Rob's death six years later. Jenny didn't think that would happen to Dare since he hadn't taken much prodding to open up.

She kept trying to figure out if he was too good to be true. So far, he seemed genuine, and that filled her with hope. Maybe her message in the bottle had brought her more than a friend. The possibility existed for something bigger, something lasting. The idea thrilled her. She liked him. She was ready for more with Dare.

An hour later, she walked into his hospital room. His bed was empty. The sheets and pillow had been stripped.

Jenny's heart seized in her chest. She struggled to draw air into her lungs. Maybe he was in the bathroom.

"Dare?"

No answer. Of course not. It was clear the room was empty.

Memories of her dad and mom hit with the force of a train, crashing into her with horrifying clarity. Her dad had passed first. She'd come into his hospital room after being with her mom in the ICU, and he was gone. Her mom had never regained consciousness and died two days later.

But that had happened years ago. She wasn't here for her parents but for Dare.

Where was he? Was his room being cleaned? Were more images being taken? Was he at physical therapy?

A hundred questions boomeranged through her brain. The room shifted, as if tilting. She reached out to grab something but found only air. She stumbled.

Her heartbeat accelerated.

Her feet felt unsteady. Her legs, too.

Oh, no. She knew what was happening.

Don't panic. Dare was fine when you left last night. He's fine now. If not, his mom would have called.

Logically, Jenny knew those things, but fear continued to grow...to take over.

Pressure grew in her chest. Her heart seemed to be doing its own thing—palpitations.

Her throat closed as if something were choking her. She trembled, not only her hands—now clammy—but her entire body.

Nightmares of walking into empty hospital rooms had plagued her for months after her parents died. The dreams returned after Rob's death, even though he'd never made it to a hospital before he died.

But here...now...it felt like she was living a dream. One that struck straight to her core.

Dare.

Her eyes burned.

Relax. Breathe. Get back in control.

A door opened.

"Jenny?"

Dare's voice.

She jerked her gaze toward him.

A nurse was pushing him into the room.

Jenny ran to him.

"You're okay." She hugged him and then touched his face as if to prove he wasn't a dream. "You're here."

"I was visiting Carlos. We had a good talk. I

needed to stay with him." Dare's gaze narrowed. He reached up to cup her face. "You're so pale. You're shaking."

The nurse came around the wheelchair to Jenny. "Let's have you sit."

"Okay." As she was led to a chair, she kept her gaze on Dare and focused on her breathing.

"Has this happened before?" the nurse asked.

She nodded once. "Not for a while. I'm...calming down now. I just thought..."

"What's going on, Jenny?" Dare asked, his voice full of concern.

"I sometimes get anxious." She sounded calmer than she felt, but she was relaxing more and more. Her pulse slowed. Tension eased from her muscles. "When you weren't here and the bed was stripped, I, um, panicked."

"Oh, babe. I'm sorry." Dare rolled the wheelchair using his good arm and leg. He leaned forward and wrapped his right arm around her. "I'm moving to another room this morning. My phone is with the stuff the orderly took, so I was going to wait here for you, but my visit went longer than expected. I thought I'd beat you here."

"Let's stay here for a few minutes more," the nurse said.

"That sounds like a plan." Dare kept hold of her.

Jenny let him. She wished he would never let go.

Twenty minutes later, Dare was settled in his new room, and the nurse had left them alone.

Questions filled his eyes, yet he'd been quiet. He didn't look tired from visiting Carlos, but Dare wasn't relaxed, either. Lines creased his forehead and around his mouth.

"Are you going to tell me what happened?" he finally asked.

The same goes for you.

She'd asked him to talk to her. It was her turn. "Yes, I probably should."

"Not probably."

He was correct. Jenny looked away.

"My parents and my brother are dead." There was no way to sugarcoat what needed to be said. "My parents were killed in a head-on collision. Rob, my little brother and Missy's husband, was a marine. He was killed in Afghanistan six years ago. IED."

Dare wrapped his arm around her, blanketing her in his warmth. "Oh, babe."

"My mom was in the ICU, so I split time between her and my dad's room. One afternoon, I went to see him and his room was empty like yours. There'd been some mix-up, but he was dead and had been moved out without anyone telling me. I had nightmares about it for a long time, but they stopped. After Rob's death, they started up again. Anxiety attacks followed. Not many, but a few, and a couple of them happened in not the best places. I've been fine for over four years, but I freaked when you weren't there this morning. Logically, I knew you were fine, but... I'm so sorry."

"Don't apologize. Fear isn't logical. And based on what happened to your family..." Dare held her tight, providing a comfort and security she'd only dreamed of feeling someday. "I'm here, and I plan to be here. With you. If the grim reaper has other ideas, I won't go without a fight. I'll do my best to show him not to mess with a ranger."

A smile tugged at the corners of her mouth. "You'd better."

He gazed into her eyes. "Anything for you."

Forget having a little crush on this man. She had a big one. She was falling hard for Dare.

He slipped his hand around her and pulled her closer. His mouth met hers in the gentlest of kisses. The tender touch made Jenny feel so special, and she leaned into him and his kiss.

"You mean so much to me." He showered kisses up her jawline until he reached her earlobe. "I don't want you to feel that kind of panic or anxiety. I'll do everything I can to keep you safe, Jenny. Make you feel safe. I promise, but I am in the military, and I get deployed. A lot. Is that going to be a problem for you?"

"Honestly, I don't know." She wasn't sure how to answer. "Everything has been happening in real time, but I have thought about the future. What you do worries me, and it might be easier if you had some other kind of job, but my parents are proof that you can just be going about your day and have something awful happen."

"So being in the military isn't a deal breaker like not believing in aliens and Bigfoot?" he joked.

"Well, when you put it that way..."

He kissed her again. "You need time to think about it. Not be pushed into a decision, okay?"

"Okay." Jenny smiled at him. "But I'm pretty sure the military isn't going to be a problem."

Her affection for this man kept growing. Jenny couldn't imagine what her life would be like without him. She didn't want to. She'd rather talk about their future together, even if that was only visiting their hometowns right now. For the first time in a long time, she wanted a relationship.

She wanted Dare.

She just hoped he wanted Jenny.

CHAPTER ELEVEN

DARE'S NEW ROOM came with a great view and a roommate. Vince Antonello was a private who'd been wounded. He'd been at the hospital for a few months. The guy was healing so slowly it didn't seem like he would ever recover, but Vince didn't seem to mind. He read books during the day when he wasn't off for treatments and talked in his sleep at night. All in all, not bad for a roomie.

His parents had needed to return to their jobs in Erie, Pennsylvania. The past two days, Dare's mom had stepped up and treated Vince like a long-lost son, and the kid was eating up the attention. She'd also baked cookies for Carlos with extra for Vince and Dare.

He'd had Jenny go with him to deliver the cookies to Carlos. The visit had been brief but proved to Dare she could handle being a military wife. Seeing the two interact—telling funny stories about him—was the proof he needed that Jenny would fit into his world just fine. He hoped she saw that, too. Only...

Vince's parents as well as Carlos' fiancée returning home had Dare thinking about Jenny. When did she need to leave? Part of him didn't want to ask the question, but he couldn't pretend she didn't have a life in Berry Lake. One that didn't include him.

He didn't even know what she did for a living. She had been here, and that was all that mattered, but now he needed to know more about her life at home.

Dare would ask what her plans were today.

Jenny entered the room with two shopping bags. She handed one to Vince and the other to Dare. "These are for you."

Dare glanced into his bag to see puzzle books, a deck of cards, and candy. "Thanks so much."

"This is great, Jenny." Vince removed a handheld electronic game. "The game will keep me busy until I get more books to read."

Dare kissed her forehead. "You shouldn't have."

"Yes, she should have," Vince countered. "I love presents."

Jenny laughed.

Dare shook his head. "I wasn't talking to you, Vince."

Vince raised a hand. "Sorry, dude. Talk away. I'm going to play my game."

Dare waited to see if Vince said anything else. He didn't.

"I'm going to have Jenny pull the curtain," Dare said. "Sorry, but I want some privacy with my girl."

"Just don't be too loud." Vince laughed.

Jenny closed the curtain that separated the two halves of the room. "Privacy, huh?"

Dare shrugged. "Do you want an audience?"

"Depends on what you have in mind."

Oh, he had lots in mind, but not now. "You're tempting me to go rogue and forget what I had planned."

"What did you have planned?"

"It's boring."

"Boring is my middle name."

Dare didn't buy that for a second. "Well, I wanted to ask about your schedule."

Her nose crinkled. "Schedule?"

He nodded. "How long are you planning to stay? It's crazy, but I've never asked when you needed to go home or about your job."

"You've had a lot going on."

She hadn't answered him. "So..."

"I'm self-employed," she said without missing a beat. "I set my own schedule and can stay as long as you need me. Missy is doing better than either of us thought she would on her own."

Okay, but Jenny hadn't completely answered his question. "What do you do for a living?"

"I'm a writer."

That was...unexpected. "What do you write?"

She wiped her palms on her jeans. "Books."

"Would I have read any?" Vince shouted.

So much for the curtain, but Dare was glad his roommate asked the question so he didn't have to.

"Have you read *Expecting the Sasquatch's Baby*? *Wanted: Sasquatch Lover*? *The Sasquatch's Runaway Bride*?"

"Can't say I've read any Bigfoot romances," Vince said. "But I may have to check one out if you wrote it."

Heat rushed up Dare's cheeks. He didn't know if Jenny was serious, but that would explain her Bigfoot fascination. "I haven't read those, but they sound...um...*interesting*."

Jenny burst out laughing. "I'm kidding."

"She got you good, dude." Vince laughed, too.

"You should have seen the expression on your face," she joked. "You're totally blushing. It's adorable."

Adorable wasn't the adjective Dare wanted her to use to describe him. "What do you really write?"

"Thrillers. I have a series called the Thorpe Files."

Vince swore. The curtain opened.

"I don't believe this," he said. "You're Jenna Ford?"

It was Jenny's turn to blush. "Jenna Ford is my pseudonym."

Dare looked at Vince. "You've read Jenny's books?"

"Who hasn't?" Vince appeared starstruck. "Ashton Thorpe is the man. They're making a movie from the first book. Can't wait to see who they pick to play Ash."

"Let's hope whoever it is does Ash proud," Jenny said.

The name of the character sounded familiar, more so than her author name. Ashton Thorpe. Where did Dare know that name?

"You have to read *Assassin Down*, dude." The excitement in Vince's voice matched the look in his eyes. "It's the first book in the series. I've read it five times. Gets better each time."

Assassin Down. Realization dawned. Dare knew that book. Carlos had loaned it to him during a deployment last year. "Is that the one where they use submarines to smuggle drugs?"

"That's it. You have to read the rest of the series," Vince added.

Dare smiled at Jenny, who seemed embarrassed.

"Looks like I've read one of your books after all."

She gave him a closemouthed smile.

"I've gotta ask. I read an interview where you called Ash your perfect man," Vince said. "How does Dare stack up?"

Dare shifted uncomfortably in his bed.

"Ash is the perfect fictional guy." She leaned over and kissed Dare. "I prefer being with this real guy better."

Just great. Ash was perfect, and Dare was real. He grimaced.

"Move over Ashton Thorpe, there's a new hero in town. Lucky you, Dare." Vince snickered. "You could wind up as Mr. Ford. Make that Sergeant Ford."

Dare stiffened. His roommate was turning into a real pain.

Jenny bit her lip. "Ford isn't my real name."

"But your readers think it is," Vince countered.

She shrugged.

"So, Jenna," Vince said. "What's it like to be a rich and famous bestselling author?"

"My name is Jenny." She toyed with the edge of the blanket on Dare's bed. "And it doesn't suck."

She spoke in a lighthearted tone, but her smile looked fake. She scratched her neck.

Dare stared at her, dumbfounded. He knew

nothing about writing or authors, but the Jenny he knew wasn't rich and famous. He thought she would deny both. But she hadn't, and he couldn't wrap his head around that.

"Cool." The way Vince nodded made him seem like he was party to a secret.

Secret.

The word echoed through Dare's mind...as did his mother's words.

Your father was the master at keeping secrets. I had to drag everything out of him.

Pressure built behind Dare's temples, and his forehead throbbed. A heaviness pressed down on him. He felt as if he were being run over by a tank.

Jenny had been keeping secrets from him since she'd arrived. Her parents. Her brother. Her job. Her...fame.

Jenny had wanted him to open up to her. He had, but she hadn't been willing to do the same. Not until he'd asked. Dare had needed to drag the words out of her tonight, just like his mom had tried to do with his father for years.

That raised a huge red flag. One that totally eclipsed Jenny wanting to stay home when he loved traveling to new places, which was the only requirement on her list he didn't meet. Roswell was something he could compromise on, as well as Bigfoot, even the traveling when he wasn't being deployed. But if he couldn't trust her to tell him things...

"Were you going to tell me about this?" Dare gritted out the words.

"Yes."

"When?"

"I don't know."

His father had said something similar when questioned by his mom. The words "I don't know" had been his dad's catchphrase. His dad had never known anything. Dare's muscles tensed into knots.

Jenny touched his shoulder. "What's wrong?"

"You've been keeping so many secrets from me." His voice sounded hoarse. "Is there anything else I should know about you?"

"I wasn't keeping secrets. You're injured. Knowing about my family or what I do wouldn't have helped you right now."

"Those things are part of who you are. Stuff that will help me know you better."

"I was trying to protect you."

"That's my job." The words burst from his mouth so fast she flinched. "Or was my job. Now..."

He stared at his arm in a cast and his leg in another cast.

Worthless. That was what he was.

Jenny was five years older than him. The age difference hadn't mattered. But add in a successful career, one that earned her a lot of money, way more than he'd ever earn in the army, and where did that leave him?

He'd never be the breadwinner. Never be able to take care of her. Not the way he wanted. Vince's statement about Dare being Mr. Ford could be what everybody would think. Dare didn't know if he could handle that.

A coldness seeped through him. He wanted to bolt, but he was stuck in bed. A sad realization made him feel empty, almost numb.

Did Jenny even need someone like him in her life?

No. The word resonated through him. She didn't need him.

She clutched his arm. "Dare, please. I'm sorry—"

"Go back to your hotel, Jenny or Jenna. Whoever you are. It's over." Dare shrugged off her touch. It was over. He'd tried to have another relationship and failed. He was finished trying. "I want to be alone."

Her lower lip quivered. "But—"

"Go."

She walked to the end of the bed and then turned. Her eyes were cold, and her skin flushed. "Before I leave, there is one more thing I haven't told you."

Dare knew it. His jaw tensed. "What?"

"I told you about my fiancé, but I left something out. He didn't only want me to pay part of his debt. He wanted me to cover the entire balance. I asked him to sign a prenuptial agreement, so I wouldn't have to pay anything. It would have also made him give up any rights to my books. He wouldn't sign, and he told me that the only reason he—or any man—would want to be with me was because of Jenna Ford. But you proved him wrong. You don't want Jenna or Jenny."

Before he could say anything, she hurried out of the room.

"Dude." Vince shook his head. "I hope you know what you're doing, because she's pissed. I have a feeling she's not coming back."

"I told her to go. I meant it. I just want to be alone."

And Dare did.

Except...he couldn't explain why his stomach churned and he felt sick.

CHAPTER TWELVE

IN THE HOSPITAL lobby, Jenny called Susan to tell her Dare was upset and she was going to her hotel. When Susan asked why, Jenny told her to talk with her son.

The drive to the hotel seemed to take twice as long as usual. Jenny focused on the road. It was the only way to keep from falling apart. A burning charcoal briquette was lodged in her throat. A weight pressed against her chest.

She parked the car and hurried inside. The first two times she inserted her key card into the lock, the door to her room wouldn't open. She tried again. The green diode illuminated.

Thank goodness.

Her shoulders sagged. She was struggling to hold herself together, but she only needed a few seconds more...

A push on the door handle, and she nearly fell into her room. Her bag slid off her shoulder. If not for her laptop inside, she would have let it fall to the carpet.

Instead, she set her tote gently on the floor.

The door closed and...

Hot tears streamed down her face. All the hurt and confusion she was feeling poured out.

She wasn't sure what had happened, but things had gone downhill fast. The finality in Dare's eyes and the harshness in his voice when he told her to leave had broken her heart. She'd never seen him like that. Not even after a bad therapy session.

He hadn't been asking her to leave his room.

Dare wanted her out of his life.

Go.

With trembling hands, Jenny pulled out her phone and called Missy.

No answer.

That brought more tears.

Between sobs, Jenny left a voice message. Most likely incoherent, but she'd tried.

With her cell still in hand, she collapsed on the bed. Her heart felt as if it were splitting into pieces. Sharp, fragmented ones that were cutting her from the inside.

Jenny's phone rang. The ringtone belonged to Missy. "Hey."

That was what Jenny had intended to say, but she had a feeling it was more of a grunt.

"What is going on?" Missy's words tumbled out one on top of the other. "I couldn't understand your message."

"I was crying."

"Because..."

"Dare and I..." Tears stung Jenny's eyes again. She stared up at the ceiling, but that didn't help. "It's over."

"What happened?"

Jenny explained how Dare's question about her schedule and job evolved into accusations of her keeping secrets and him telling her to leave.

"Are you sure it's over?" Missy asked. "I know what happened with Grant has kept you from getting serious about anybody, but I've never heard you talk about a man like you talk about Dare."

"I was ready to pursue something more with Dare. I...I love him."

"Oh, Jenny..."

"Love is the only thing that explains why I'm falling apart right now, but I was falling for him before this happened. And everything since then confirms it."

Jenny hiccupped. Her breath stuttered, and she wiped her tears before continuing.

"Dare took me to meet one of his guys earlier. Carlos. He's a corporal. In his early twenties. Nice guy, who might be paralyzed, but as soon as Dare walked into the room, Carlos lit up. Watching Dare be there for and interact with Carlos showed me how special Dare is. I never thought about dating someone in the military after what happened with Rob, but that wouldn't stop me from being with Dare. It's part of who he is, and he gives so much of himself. Oh, Missy... I wanted some of that. I thought I had it."

"Let's figure this out." Missy sounded like a woman with a mission. "Maybe you misunderstood."

"Dare said it's over. He used those exact words." Jenny sniffled. "It's so crazy. I always thought men only wanted to be with Jenna Ford. I never thought I'd be dumped because I *was* her. Losing him... It hurts so bad."

"I'm so sorry. That's what sucks about love. It's inherently risky. There's zero control. You may get hurt a little or a lot, but in the end, loving another person is worth it."

Jenny stiffened. "How can you say that? The way I feel isn't worth anything except a bunch of heartache. And losing Rob almost destroyed you."

"Yes, it did, and I wish with every beat of my heart that he were still here, but loving him was worth the pain and grief. Even knowing what would happen to Rob, and that there'd be this gaping hole where my heart should be, I wouldn't change anything."

"I haven't even known Dare long. But the feelings seem real."

"They are real. You told me grief has no set time frame. Neither does love. Once it's there, you know, but you also can't force another to love you back." A long exhale sounded. "Maybe you need to walk away and let Dare figure out what you mean to him."

Jenny almost laughed. "You mean the 'if you love them set them free' routine."

"Yes, he may come back."

"And if he doesn't?"

"There's going to be one spoiled kitten in Berry Lake, and you always have Ash."

Ash.

But for the first time, Ashton Thorpe wasn't enough. He had been before because he was safe and did whatever she wanted. So what if Ash was make believe? He'd been all she needed.

Until receiving that email from DOR.

Dare, however, was everything Jenny wanted in a man. She'd believed his finding her message in the bottle was meant to be.

Fate, kismet, serendipity, whatever this was called.

She loved Dare.

The last man she'd said the words "I love you" to

had been Grant. He'd never put anyone first, including Jenny. She'd thought she understood what love was, but her feelings—her love—for Grant had never been this strong or felt so right as it did with Dare.

What was she going to do?

Nothing.

A boulder settled in the pit of her stomach.

Missy was correct. Jenny couldn't force Dare to love her in return. He had told her to leave, and that was what she would do.

But first, she needed to cry and then sleep.

****

The next morning, Dare was so tired from not sleeping he wondered if the nurse could give him an IV of coffee. He couldn't stop thinking about the emotions that had crossed Jenny's face last night—confusion, hurt, anger. But he'd done the right thing.

"We can play a game of cards," Vince said. He'd been trying to be supportive, but Dare wished his roommate would read a book or something. "I have an occupational therapy session soon, but when I get back."

"Sure." When Vince returned, maybe Dare would be asleep.

Vince left, and Dare's mom entered the room with muffins and coffee from the cafeteria. She set them on his bed tray. Two cups, not three. That made him shift.

The circles under her eyes probably matched his. "You need sleep, Mom."

"I'll take a nap later, but you don't look good and Jenny is hurting." His mom ignored the food and paced. "Call her."

"I told you it's over." Dare dragged his hand through his hair. "She's been keeping secrets from me. Just like Dad."

"Jenny Hanford is nothing like your father."

Dare pressed his lips together.

"You really want to compare her to your dad?"

"It's true."

"Not even close." His mother walked to the bed. "Your dad wouldn't have dropped everything and flown halfway across the country for anyone. He wouldn't have slept on an uncomfortable chair or stayed there while you napped because you wanted him to hold your hand. I've heard of Jenna Ford, and she's a big name. A few times, I saw her with a notepad or a laptop, but that was only while you slept. You know what that means? She put her writing on hold for you."

Dare didn't say anything. He couldn't. "She kept

what she did from me. I only found out about her parents and her brother because she had an anxiety attack."

"Which should tell you how affected she was by those events."

"I told you how she wanted me to open up. To say what I was thinking. Spill my guts."

"Because she cared."

"Not enough to do the same."

"Did it ever occur to you that Jenny might not have told you those things because you were injured, recovering, and had too much going on?" his mom asked.

I was trying to protect you.

That was what Jenny had said last night. "I don't need to be protected."

"Everybody needs that. Even you, Mr. Tough Guy." His mom touched his hand. "You had to grow up fast when your father left. You stepped into the man-of-the-house role without any direction. I'm sorry that was forced on you, but you handled it like a champ. Your sisters and I needed you. But letting your boyhood memories of a man who was a poor excuse for a father ruin what you have with Jenny would be a mistake."

His mom shook her head, looking upset.

"Last night, you had an audience, and things escalated quickly. Why not talk to Jenny alone and see if you can work things out? Explain why you were so upset when you thought she was keeping secrets from you."

"I could, but..." His insides twisted like the bit on a drill. "There's more going on than her not telling me things. Even if we could work that out, someone so successful wouldn't want me."

"Oh, sweetie, that is not true. Money and fame don't make a person happy."

"Jenny doesn't need me to take care of her."

"What does it matter if a woman is successful? That doesn't change how she feels about you. That doesn't lessen who you are or what you do. Please don't let your male ego get in the way." His mother's tone was hard. She sounded disappointed in him, and that sliced Dare to the core. "Jenny lights up when you are in the room. She laughs and smiles and cares. That's because of you. You're special, Dare, and I have no doubt that she is absolutely crazy about you."

He wanted to believe his mom. "But what if Jenny sees her life going another way? What if she wants a different ending to our story? What if she'd rather have someone more like the characters in her books?"

"That's something you need to talk about. Don't

decide for her."

"I did last night." The realization of what he'd done nearly knocked him over, even though he was lying in bed. He'd thought nothing could match the hurt that Kayla and Brock had caused when they'd cheated.

Dare was wrong. Only...this had been his fault.

"I screwed up. What was I thinking?"

His mom's expression softened. "Love isn't logical, honey."

His eyes burned. He slammed his fists into the mattress. "I have to make this right."

If he didn't do something to get Jenny back, he was going to lose it. Big time.

Running after her wasn't an option. He couldn't walk without help. He couldn't drive. He couldn't do...anything.

Hamilton's words echoed through Dare's head.

When have you let that stop you before, O'Rourke?

Never.

Dare wouldn't stop now. Surrendering wasn't how it was done. He would fight for what he wanted, for her.

But how?

Think, O'Rourke.

There had to be something he could do.

Rangers lead the way.

The motto sounded in his head. Maybe he couldn't do something on his own, but if he asked for help...

He'd lost the most important person in his life when Jenny left last night. What more did he have to lose?

"Mom, do you think you could do something for me?"

"Of course, honey, what do you need?"

"I need you and Carlos. Maybe Vince, too." The guy was annoying, but Dare needed to stack the odds in his favor.

He couldn't lose Jenny. He wouldn't.

****

Jenny's hands shook as she packed her suitcase. She needed to pull herself together if she was going to visit the Alamo before she headed to the airport.

A beep sounded. Her cell phone.

Her heart leaped, thinking the text might be from Dare, but when she checked her phone, she saw it was from his mom. Not that she didn't like Susan, but disappointment clawed at Jenny's heart as if she were being jabbed by small, razor-sharp talons.

She shook her head. It was going to be a long day. Week. Month. Year...

Susan: *Favor to ask. Any chance you could get an autographed copy of one of your books and drop it off for Carlos today? Turns out he's a bigger fan of yours than Vince and has been having a rough morning.*

Jenny: *Sure. I don't fly out until tonight. I'll swing by a bookstore. I can pick up one for Vince, too.*

Susan: *Thanks. Text me when you arrive. I want to say goodbye.*

Jenny: *Okay.*

Three hours later, Jenny arrived at the hospital with a box full of books for Carlos, Vince, and the other patients. Hopefully, the staff would pass them out. That was the least she could do for the service members who made so many sacrifices and put their lives on the line.

Like Dare.

Don't think about him.

If only she could stop.

With a sigh, she texted Susan from the lobby, and then Jenny sat at a table, pulled a pen from her purse, and autographed the books. The first set of the Thorpe Files novels was personalized to Carlos. The second set would go to Vince. On the other books, she wrote a greeting followed by her signature and the date.

Susan still hadn't arrived after Jenny had signed them all. She looked around. The place was crowded, as usual. She'd spent so much time at the hospital these past weeks she couldn't imagine not coming here tomorrow.

Except she'd be home in Berry Lake by then. She looked forward to seeing Missy and the kittens.

"There you are." All smiles, Susan walked up to her. "Thanks so much for doing this."

"Not a problem." And it wasn't. Jenny was happy to help. "The books are good to go. The two stacks facing the different directions are for Carlos and Vince. Just check the title page to see who it belongs to. The other books are single copies the nurses can pass out to patients."

"How thoughtful of you, but why don't you hand them out yourself?" Susan asked. "You have time, right?"

The Alamo tour wasn't scheduled until later. "Yes, but to be honest, I'd rather not see Dare."

Susan touched Jenny's arm. "I understand, but please don't worry about him."

If only she could stop. "Okay. Where to first?"

"Carlos' room."

Jenny donned the yellow disposable scrubs, mask, and gloves, and then entered Carlos' room with the books. A curtain had been pulled, making the room seem smaller than the last time she was here.

"Hey," she said. "I wanted to stop by and say hi. I brought you a couple of books."

"Thanks." For someone having a rough day, Carlos didn't look so bad. He wasn't smiling, but he didn't have a frown or a sad expression on his face. "You're one of my favorite authors."

Now he was making *her* feel better. Grinning, she sat in the chair next to his bed. She put the box on the floor, removed his books, and placed them on the bed tray. "Thank you. You made my day."

"It's the truth," Carlos said without hesitation. "Ash is a badass."

"He is, but so are you guys."

"Sergeant O'Rourke's the real deal."

Jenny felt a pang. Okay, the words hit her like a sucker punch, but she recognized how much Carlos respected his sergeant and looked up to Dare. "Yes, he is. Don't tell anyone I said this, but Ashton Thorpe can't hold a candle to Darragh O'Rourke."

A smile tugged at Carlos' lips. "You sound

certain."

"I am," she said with confidence. "Ash is a man's man, but there's a reason he never gets the girl. He doesn't deserve her."

Carlos winked. "I thought Ash ended up alone so you could write another story with a new love interest."

"That, too." She laughed. "But it also works with his character."

Carlos' eyebrows drew together. "How?"

She thought for a moment. "Well, Ash acts as a lone wolf. He has no team or comrades to rely on or console when things go south. He moves on to the next mission without realizing the pains—emotional and physical—of those he left behind. Ash never has to make sacrifices, not like Dare, and while Dare might not save the world as Ash does in each book, Dare saves individuals, and that's equally as important."

"Sounds like you know the two men well."

She shrugged. "One I created and control. He's alone because I say so. The other is a wild card. Unfortunately, he's choosing to be alone, and there's nothing I can do about that."

That was probably too much information to give the young corporal, but the words were out before she could stop them.

"Sometimes, even heroes mess up. Thanks for the books, Jenny. These are copies I won't be loaning out," Carlos said. He picked up and put on a pair of headphones before pointing behind her.

She turned.

The curtain was open.

Dressed in yellow scrubs, Dare sat in his wheelchair. Squatchy was tucked in next to him.

Her mouth gaped. No words would come.

Dare wasn't a small man by any means, but sitting there with a worried expression and a stuffed animal made him look more vulnerable than he had the night she'd arrived in San Antonio.

He rolled himself toward her. Well, as far as he could before the bed got in his way.

"I'm no hero. More like an idiot. I screwed up big time. The stuff I said to you was wrong. I'm sorry." His contrite voice matched his sad eyes, and all she wanted to do was put a smile back on his face. "The last thing I wanted—want—to do is hurt you, Jenny. But things— I—got out of control so fast, but I finally figured out why I got upset like that."

"I love you," they said at the same time.

His mouth curved upward into a breathtaking grin. "At least we agree on that."

Smiling, she stood. "We should be able to find

more."

Tension evaporated from him. "I was scared. I saw us going one way—my way—and then I found out about your writing. For some reason, it hit on all my insecurities. I was positive I'd never be enough for you. That you wouldn't want or need me."

The sincerity in his voice wrapped around her heart and squeezed tight. "Oh, Dare."

"There is something I haven't told you yet. My dad... He kept secrets from my mom, and that tore them apart. I used you not telling me stuff as an excuse to protect myself and my ego. That's why I told you to go. I'm so sorry. I'll do whatever it takes for you to forgive me."

Her heart swelled with hope. She wanted this to work out. There was only one thing to say. "I forgive you."

He reached out to her, and she was at his side in an instant. "I'm sorry for not telling you more right away, but I wanted you to like Jenny before you found out about Jenna and the books."

"I fell for your words, Jenny, not Jenna's. What you wrote in the emails and texts made me want to take a chance on a relationship again. Looking back, I'm sure I was in love with you before I'd ever even seen you."

He took her hand, rubbing his thumb softly over the back of it. His expression was tender, hopeful.

Her heart melted.

"I love you, Jenny Hanford. I love Jenna Ford, too, because she's part of you. I promise you I'm not like that other guy. Just like I know I'm not going to walk in on you having sex with my best friend or some other guy. What happened with those people is in the past. That's where they belong. But for us…"

"I…I just want to be with you."

"I want the same thing, sweetheart."

He pulled her toward his mouth.

His kiss started off gently as he moved his lips over hers, but the intensity changed. Heat flared. She didn't care.

The kiss spoke of his love and desire for her. It claimed her as his and gave her all of him.

He drew back. "Have your lawyer draw up that agreement. I want you to have it ready because as soon as I can get down on one knee to propose—and I hope it won't take me long to heal enough—I'm signing it. Don't even have to read it."

"Just like that?"

Dare nodded once. "You wouldn't ask if it wasn't important to you, so why not? A piece of paper isn't going to keep us together, and another one won't drive us apart. We're the ones who have to put in the effort to make things work."

"I'll do whatever it takes."

"Good, because right now, we have to go to my room. When you see Vince, act surprised."

She drew back. "Why surprised?"

"Because he's wearing a Bigfoot costume."

Jenny let out a startled laugh. "What?" She didn't even know where to start with that information. "Why?"

"That was the second phase of my plan to get you back if this didn't work."

"It worked, Sergeant," Carlos said, even though he was still wearing headphones. "Perfect execution."

"It was that." Jenny grinned. "But Bigfoot?"

Dare shrugged. "None of us could fit into the alien costume. Not even my mom."

This man was perfect for her. So were his friends and family. Jenny kissed him hard on the lips. "I love you, Dare O'Rourke."

"I love you." He saluted. "Soul mate and one true love reporting for duty."

A peace settled over her, one that she'd never expected to feel with her emotions exploding like fireworks over this man she loved. "At ease, soldier."

A message in a bottle had brought Dare into her

world. He was her dream hero come to life. No other man—real or fictional—could compare.

Her future was shining in his eyes. She smiled. "We'll be adding another happy ending to those who tossed a bottle in the ocean."

He brushed his lips over her hair. "The happiest of endings, and one that includes a cuddly, cute kitten. What do you think of the name Yeti?"

* * * * *

I hope you enjoyed reading **Jenny**. Want more of these characters? To read more about Mitch and Lizzy Hamilton (and get an update on Jenny and Dare), look for my short read **Sweet Holiday Wishes**. If you want to find out what happened to Josh Cooper (and read about Jenny and Dare's wedding), check out **Sweet Beginnings**.

TO HEAR ABOUT FUTURE RELEASES,
SIGN UP FOR MY NEWSLETTER!

I send newsletters two to three times each month with info about new releases, sales, freebies, and giveaways. To subscribe go to www.melissamcclone.com.

IF YOU ENJOYED READING THIS BOOK,
PLEASE LEAVE A REVIEW.

Honest reviews by readers like yourself help bring attention to books. A review can be as short or as detailed as you like. Thank you so much!

Meet the Beach Brides:

MEG (Julie Jarnagin)

TARA (Ginny Baird)

NINA (Stacey Joy Netzel)

CLAIR (Grace Greene)

JENNY (Melissa McClone)

LISA (Denise Devine)

HOPE (Aileen Fish)

KIM (Magdalena Scott)

ROSE (Shanna Hatfield)

LILY (Ciara Knight)

FAITH (Helen Scott Taylor)

AMY (Raine English)

LIsa

Beach Brides Series

by

Denise Devine

PROLOGUE

LISA'S MESSAGE IN a bottle...

To Whom it may concern,

I'm an adventurous girl, who'd love to see the world, but I don't have the money or the time.

If I met someone, though, who liked to travel for fun, he'd become a best friend of mine.

I love the mountains, the seas, the rocks and the trees, and the Cairo Museum of Antiquities.

I've never seen a polar bear, or visited The World's Fair, or climbed the Eiffel Tower in France.

I want to see pyramids, ride a tram atop a rainforest, and visit Spain to watch the Flamenco dance.

Do you like piña coladas and strolling in the

rain?

Is there a special place in the world you'd love to see again?

If you're a guy who loves to fly, or cruise on the mighty sea, then give me a shout, tell me what you're all about, 'cause you might be the one for me.

IslandGirl#1@...

CHAPTER ONE

Enchanted Island, East Caribbean
The Month of July

LISA KAYE SIPPED her cabernet and stared at the blank page in front of her, wondering how to compose a message to a man she'd never met.

The twelve women in her group, The Romantic Hearts Book Club, had chosen to spend their last night vacationing together on Enchanted Island working on a "spur-of-the-moment" project. The group had read and discussed many romance novels since the club's inception and each woman had a favorite hero from the book of her choice, a man she would love to call her own. Lisa didn't know who had suggested the concept, but after a spirited discussion and a couple rounds of cocktails, the group had concluded that each woman would compose a personal message to her "dream hero," stuff it into a bottle and throw the bottle in the Caribbean ocean. In Lisa's opinion, the chance of anyone—much less the perfect man—finding her bottle and taking the message seriously seemed ludicrous, but everyone else had agreed to do it so Lisa decided to go along with the plan.

After dinner, the women gathered at the poolside bar to take in the balmy air of their last evening together at the Hideaway Cove Resort. The atmosphere vibrated through the open-air pavilion with the jaunty, percussion-like sounds of Reggae music played on steel drums. A small group of people played a lively game of volleyball in the adjacent pool.

Sitting at a round table for two, Lisa rested her hand on her chin and tried to come up with something clever to put in her message. The harder she tried to concentrate, though, the more her mind stubbornly refused to cooperate.

The young woman sitting across from her sipped a glass of chablis. "How are you doing on your message," Clair inquired as the warm Caribbean breeze ruffled a few wisps of hair from her French braid. Her dark locks contrasted richly against her magenta sundress. "Are you making any progress?"

Lisa slid the blank paper toward Clair and sighed. "I can't even get started. How are you coming along with yours?"

"I need to work on mine, but I'm not putting a lot of effort into it. I don't see the point in writing a message to a complete stranger when I already have a dream hero back at home." Clair's fine brows drew together in annoyance as she leaned closer. "If you ask me, the idea is pretty silly."

Lisa nodded. "It's risky, too. What if the wrong person gets hold of my bottle and begins to stalk me on line?"

Clair's brown eyes widened with an incredulous stare. "You're not going to put your personal email address on it, are you?"

Lisa shook her head. "No way, I've created a new one on enchantedisland.net specifically for this purpose and I'm not using my real name. If anyone replies, I'll know the person found the bottle."

"That's good," Clair replied, looking relieved. "I did the same thing. I don't want anyone getting hold of my personal information." She slid the sheet of paper back to Lisa. "Think of your ideal man and write to him."

Lisa chuckled. "As a kid, I had a crush on Indiana Jones. I used to run around the house wearing my dad's Fedora, a brown vest and carrying my sister's lunge whip, pretending that Indy and I were exploring archeological wonders together. I've read quite a few books with that type of character and I've loved them all." She doodled on the paper, drawing a crude outline of a small treasure map. "Sometimes I wish I'd pursued a college degree in archaeology instead of business administration. Maybe I'd be doing something more exciting with my life now instead of supervising the Personal Lines Department of an insurance agency."

Clair grabbed a business card off another table and flipped it over to the blank side. "This will work. Do you have a pen I could borrow?"

She handed Clair a pen and went back to work, racking her brain to come up with something suitable.

After twenty minutes, another glass of wine and three sheets of paper, Lisa showed her message to Clair. "It sounds more like a Dr. Seuss book than a memo to Mr. Right, but that's the best I can do."

Clair picked up the sheet and scanned the words. "It's cute. And totally you. I like it." She slid it back across the table. "What are you using for a bottle?"

"Gosh, I forgot to get one." Lisa took the sheet and began to fold the paper into a narrow strip. "I wonder if I can get a beer bottle and a cork from the bar."

But when she went to the bar and asked for a bottle to use, the bartender refused, warning her that the resort forbade throwing any trash into the bay. She'd purchased an antique bottle from a small curio shop in the island's historic downtown area, but she certainly didn't want to use that one. The triangular cobalt bottle had attracted her, embossed with "Owl Drug Company" and a figure of an owl sitting upon a mortar with one claw clutching the pestle. The shopkeeper had remarked that he came by the bottle after a local resident had fished it out of the bay. She hated the thought of throwing it back in there!

Unless I don't actually toss the bottle—just make it look like I threw it...

The early evening sun dipped low in the sky, hanging over the endless horizon of the Caribbean ocean like a crimson ball of fire. The twelve women laughed and talked as they walked through a grove of palms in an undeveloped area next to the resort. Tara and Meg led the way along the well-trodden trail to a remote strip of shoreline, far enough from the resort so no one in the area could see them tossing their bottles into the water. Jenny and Faith were next in line. They vowed to organize another group getaway and smacked their palms together in agreement. Behind them, Nina and Hope joined in, laughing as they offered a few suggestions.

Lisa and Clair hung back, trailing the group so they could chat.

"Ouch! Wait a minute." Clair stopped and pulled off one of her silver flip-flops to remove a tiny fragment of coral stuck in the ball of her foot. She looked up. "Are you leaving tomorrow with us or are you staying on to visit with your aunt?"

"I came a few days early and spent time with her," Lisa said as they stood on the sandy trail. "She wants me to move here permanently to take over her bed and breakfast hotel."

Her Aunt Elsie Dubois lived in a large pink and white house on the edge of the island's historic business district. Lisa had poignant childhood memories of time spent here, roaming the cobblestone streets of "old town" Morganville and playing on the beaches with her cousins. The thought of living here permanently tugged at her heartstrings, but...

"Are you serious?" Clair slipped her flip-flop back on and resumed walking. "That sounds like a dream come true! Are you considering it?"

Lisa sighed with regret, knowing an opportunity

like the one Aunt Elsie had figuratively handed to her on a silver platter would never come along again. "I'd love to accept the offer, but I have too many ties back home to just drop everything and move here." She leaned close to Clair to keep their conversation private. "The last time I talked to my guy on the phone he said he had something important to tell me." She didn't know for sure, but she had the feeling Rob planned to surprise her with an engagement ring. He said he didn't want to talk about it until they were together again. What else could it be? She smiled to herself. The thought of one day becoming Rob Mancuso's wife made her heart brim with hope. "I can't wait to get back to West Palm Beach."

Clair gave her a brief, knowing smile. "I've had a great time here, but I'm getting a little antsy to get home, too."

Though she didn't say any more, Lisa understood that Clair missed the "hero" in her life and wanted to see him again.

They walked out of the palm grove and along the rocky shore until they reached an area that looked suitable to toss their bottles.

"Okay, everyone," Tara said as the group lined up. "On the count of three, throw 'em in."

Claire shook her head and mumbled, "Here goes

nothing."

Lisa drew the small blue bottle from her purse that held her message. She stood poised to throw it, but intended to merely go through the motion then quickly slip it back into her purse before anyone noticed.

"One...two...three!"

An assortment of glass in a blend of colors, sizes and shapes flew through the air and dropped into the ocean in a succession of loud plunks and splashes. Lisa clutched her bottle and swung her arm, but the bottle had something slippery on it. The oily liquid squished through her fingers. The cap on the sunscreen lotion she carried in her purse must have loosened and leaked all over everything. Darn! The bottle suddenly flew from her hand and sailed through the air like a missile then disappeared into the water, leaving only a circular wave of ripples in its wake.

Shocked, she stared across the surface of the aqua water, disappointed that she would never see that bottle again.

ABOUT THE AUTHOR

USA Today bestselling author Melissa McClone has written over forty-five sweet contemporary romance novels and been nominated for Romance Writers of America's RITA® Award. She lives in the Pacific Northwest with her husband, three children, two spoiled Norwegian Elkhounds, and cats who think they rule the house. They do! If you'd like to learn more about Melissa, please visit her website www.melissamcclone.com or email her at melissa@melissamcclone.com. You can find Melissa at her Facebook page, @melissamcclonebooks and her McClone Troopers Reader Facebook Group, @groups/McCloneTroopers or connect with her on Twitter, @melissamcclone and Instagram, @melmcclone.

OTHER BOOKS BY MELISSA MCCLONE

STANDALONE

A farmer finds more than help when he hires a consultant to help his business grow...
Carter's Cowgirl

A matchmaking aunt wants her nephew to find love under the mistletoe...
The Christmas Window

SERIES
All series stories are standalone, but past characters may show up.

Mountain Rescue Series
Finding love in Hood Hamlet with a little help from Christmas magic...
His Christmas Wish
Her Christmas Secret
Her Christmas Kiss
His Second Chance
His Christmas Family

One Night to Forever Series
Can one night change your life...and your relationship status?
Fiancé for the Night
The Wedding Lullaby

Beach Brides and Indigo Bay Sweet Romance Series
A mini-series within two multi-author series...
Jenny
Sweet Holiday Wishes
Sweet Beginnings

Ever After Series
Happily ever after reality TV style...
The Honeymoon Prize
The Cinderella Princess
Christmas in the Castle

Love at the Chocolate Shop Series
Three siblings find love thanks to Copper Mountain Chocolate...
A Thankful Heart
The Valentine Quest
The Chocolate Touch

The Bar V5 Ranch Series
Fall in love at a dude ranch in Montana...
Home for Christmas
Mistletoe Magic
Kiss Me, Cowboy
Mistletoe Wedding
A Christmas Homecoming